To Kara,

From the desk of
Author
Cherisse M Havlicek

Love = Family

Cherisse

2019

CHERISSE M HAVLICEK

Justice for Joshua

A Present / Past Saga

by

Cherisse M Havlicek

CHERISSE M HAVLICEK

This novel, is a work of fiction. The Cheyenne's 1500-mile Exodus and subsequent Settler Massacre actually took place. I have taken my imaginary characters and interspersed them with the names of real people affected as to give life to this account. It is done to, hopefully, enlighten my audience to an important event in history. The characters and events in the 1939 story are all the work of my imagination, for entertainment purposes. Any resemblance to actual persons, living or dead or actual events is purely coincidental.

DEDICATION

I would like to dedicate this story to our Native American Indians. All Tribes of every nation, historically, suffered from the expansion of the new Americans and the promises of the White Man, that were not kept. This story covers the Cheyenne hardships during the period known as the Kansas-Cheyenne War of 1878. I hope to have shed a small light on this sad episode of our American story.

ACKNOWLEDGMENTS

I must thank all those patient family members and others that have heard and helped me work through this fictional story. I have many family and friends who have taken on the task of reading my writing, pre-publication. You have steered me with your comments and insights and I could not have written this novel without you.

I must, especially, acknowledge my husband, Allan Havlicek. He may not be able to help with the story, at this point, but I know that he is behind me all the way.

ONE

"Will you be going back to Lawrence? If not, where will you be staying?"

Joshua just looks at him, blankly. Sullivan comes into the room. "Sir?" He asks.

"Mr. Lewis is leaving, Sullivan, please show him out. Joshua? Where can I reach you?"

"I assumed I would be staying here. Can I not stay in a separate bedroom? Lock me in, until you have her permission to let me out, if you must, but don't ask me to leave, PLEASE!"

"Out of the question. You cannot stay here. Sullivan, help Joshua off the sofa." Sullivan grabs his arm and with little effort brings Joshua to a standing position. "Don't make Sullivan get rough with you. Be a gentleman and leave, please Joshua. Go back to Lawrence. Or stay the night with Matthew Masters or Mark Collins. I or Juliet Helen, will call you there, tomorrow."

Sullivan has hands on Joshua, again. Joshua is trying to free himself. "Why are you doing this, Grant? This makes no sense! This isn't fair. I am her husband! Grant! Grant!" He calls as he is being pushed out of the house.

When the front door is shut in his face, he screams, "Grant, I will make you pay for this. This isn't right! She's my wife! Let me in!!" Joshua starts banging on the door. "Grant, I will make you pay for this!!!" He continues this useless action for about twenty minutes. He feels like a fool. He knows he'd better leave before Grant calls the police on him. He cannot believe he has been kicked out of the house for no apparent reason.

This situation started on the Colonel's Birthday. . .

October 31st, 1939
Tuesday In Lawrence, Kansas

She can <u>still</u> see the Colonel sitting at the large marble counter, of the diner-style kitchen, eating his half a sandwich and sneaking the crusts to his dog, Robbie. She looks over to the sink, where Robbie's dog bed lay. He is watching her with his head on the pillow. When their eyes meet, he raises his head, just a little, but puts it back down with a sigh. "Oh boy, I miss him too. He would have been eighty years old today." She goes to the old dog and bends to pet him. Robbie's tail gives half a wag. "Things just are not the same, are they?" She asks, as if she were expecting an answer. She straightens up and lets out her own sad sigh.

"Anna, you can't let the day get you down." Henry has walked into the kitchen without her hearing him.

He has their daughter, Clara Beth, on his hip. As soon as she sees her mama, the two-year-old squirms out of her daddy's arms and runs to Anna. "Mama, up?" She says as she holds out her arms, which tugs at her mother's heart. "Mama, peas?"

Anna smiles and bends down to pick-up her precious little girl. "It's Mama, *please,* Clara. Can you say *please*?"

Clara nods her head, eagerly. "Peas! Peas, peas, peas!" This makes both her parents laugh and Henry comes over to take both his girls in his arms.

Anna looks at Henry. "What are we going to do with her?" She asks while shaking her head in disbelief.

"Love her, keep her and never let her go." He kisses Clara on the forehead and then Anna on the lips. When their lips part, Clara reaches up and takes Anna's face and gives her a kiss, too.

"Wuv Mama, wuv Da-Da." She says simply then begins to squirm out of their arms and she goes to Robbie and gives him a kiss on the forehead, also. "Wuv Wobbie, too." Then she sits down next to him and pets him. She is only there for a few seconds and she is up again and goes to her little toy box next to the laundry room door and starts rooting through it for something to play with. When she finds a small doll, she sits down and cuddles it. "Wuv Dolly. I the Mommy. She the baby." She says to her parents with authority. Then she forgets they are in the room as she pretends to feed her baby with a little empty baby bottle.

Henry has his arm around Anna's waist still, as they cannot look away from their pride and joy. "She looks more and more like you every day, Anna. Same heart shaped face, same beautiful brown eyes, same light brown color hair. We are going to have our hands full when the fellas start to come a-courtin'," he laughs.

"We can avoid that by arranging her marriage like our fathers did. I never had anyone 'come a-courtin', except you." Anna smiles. Their fathers, Judd and Frank, boyhood friends, decided for them that they would be perfect for each other.

They were both very upset at the notion because even though they were childhood best friends, themselves, they had been separated for years and did not know each other anymore. Henry had started to see Anna's sister in secret when he was told he was to be engaged to Anna. He argued with his father that he was an adult and did not need his father to be his match-maker. Those were complicated times but his father was right all along. Anna was and always will be, his one true love. "If only we can pick as well as your Pa and my Da did." Henry gives Anna a squeeze, then let's go. "What are you going to do today, Anna?"

"Oh, I don't know. Bake a little, potty-train Clara, make lunch and dinner, hunt water buffalo." She says it with no enthusiasm. She is back at the sink to dry the fresh washed dishes. Even with little Clara up and walking, it seems like a very lazy day without the Colonel to look after. She was his caretaker for four years, until his passing in April. "What are you going to do today?"

"Joshua wants me to order the seed for next year's crops, while he does the payroll for the last of the seasonal workers."

Henry works as Joshua's right hand man at Legacy Plantation. The plantation has been in the Lewis family for five generations and it produces several vegetable crops, sunflower seeds, wheat and cattle on the thousands of acres that make up the family business. Joshua's sister, Carolyn, who was running the farm while Joshua was still in college had offered Henry a job the day before he and Anna were wed three years ago.

The wedding took place in the front parlor of this large Colonial style home, just days after Henry found out that his Anna was still alive. The morning after Henry formally asked Anna to marry him in 1935, she was kidnapped, beaten, raped and left for dead on the outskirts of this very plantation which is one hundred and forty miles from where their families were living. She was missing and presumed dead for a whole year but Henry never stopped looking for her.

Carolyn had found Anna's naked, bloody, beaten and unconscious body the day after the attack. She was in a coma for a long while and when she woke up, she had amnesia. Carolyn started to call her Rosanne and when she was to be released from the hospital, Carolyn and Joshua agreed to bring her to their home. During that long year, Rosanne got stronger, and she started to take care of their grandfather, the Colonel and make extraordinary meals.

Though 'large and in charge' during his prime of life, this retired Colonel of the U.S. Cavalry was a frail and confused shadow of his former self. He liked to roam the house at night then slept on and off all day, he was always cold and had a hard time keeping track of the fact that his two grandchildren were grown-ups. He and his wife Julia took in their little grandchildren to raise when their only son Kevin and his wife were killed. The Colonel also struggled with the memory of his wife's passing. He would always talk about her as if she were in the next room and had to be reminded that she had been gone since Carolyn and Joshua were thirteen and eleven.

Henry's voice breaks through Anna's thoughts. "Anna, are you going to be okay, today? I feel that you are mourning the loss of the Colonel more than his grandchildren, and there is no doubt that they loved him."

"I will be fine, Henry. It's just, I don't know, he is with me today. Dominating my thoughts. He saved my life more than once, don't forget." The Colonel helped her through the devastating loss of her baby girl, during the year she was Rosanne. Then two years ago, the Colonel killed the man who had originally attacked her and who was then, trying to kill her newborn, Clara.

"I have been thankful to him and this family for saving you with every breath I have drawn in since I heard you were alive, my Anna." He crosses back to her and takes her in his arms. "He wouldn't want you to be sad. Remember him always but not with sadness. Now cheer up!"

"I can make that an order, if you like." A female voice says behind them. They turn to see Carolyn Lewis James, the newlywed of Professor Edward James standing in the doorway. She hired Anna and Henry but is more like an adopted sister. "I know Grandfather would want us to carry on and not mope about the house." She turns to the toddler. "Not when there is this sweet little one to dote on. Clara Beth, come to your Auntie Carolyn." She bends down and holds out her arms and without hesitation, Clara stands up and runs to her.

"Auntie, see baby. I the mommy! I wuv her." She happily shows Carolyn her doll.

"What is your baby's name, Clara?"

"Dolly. She pretty?" She holds the doll out for Carolyn to see.

"Not nearly as pretty, as you are, little girl."

"I not little, I the Mama!" She defiantly squirms out of Carolyn's hands and goes back to playing with her toys.

Carolyn shrugs her shoulders, "She is getting quite the little personality, isn't she? I still cannot believe that she is two." She turns back to Anna. Carolyn is shorter that Anna but her stature and the air about her gives you the feeling she is in command. She has let her dark auburn hair get long and she is now wearing it twisted up on top of her head. "Now, as for you, I think you should take the day off, both of you. I talked with Joshua about this a few minutes ago and he said you can do the ordering tomorrow, Henry. Take your wife away from here. If you want it to be just the two of you, I will very gladly watch my niece." Anna has insisted that Carolyn and Joshua are her adopted siblings since they found her, paid all her medical bills and gave her a home when she had no place to go.

Anna looks to Henry. "We could go up for the day to EL Dorado and see my family." She smiles from ear to ear. "That would be very nice, wouldn't it, Henry?"

"Unfortunately, Carolyn, we are not allowed near the city limits of EL Dorado without little Clara Beth." He nods to his little girl. "So you lose out on babysitting privileges." He gives her a wink and mouths, a 'thank-you', then turns to Anna. "What are you waiting for? Get on the phone and make sure your family is ready for us!"

Anna practically runs to the dining room, where the downstairs phone is kept on the sideboard. Henry walks over to Carolyn and gives her a hug. "You know how to cheer her up, right quick. Are you going to be okay, today?" He is referring to her own mourning of the man that raised her.

"I was thinking of reading Gram Beth's entries the year that the Colonel meets his Julia for the first time in years. It would mean skipping ahead a few books because that took place in 1879." Carolyn is referring to her great-grandmother's forty-plus journals that they discovered in a trunk in the attic two years ago. They were the Colonel's mother's and she wrote in them almost every night for dozens of years. They also have the letters saved in the Colonel's boot locker that were from his Julia to him while he was on his campaigns. Julia, herself saved every letter sent to her. Anna and Carolyn spent two days getting them organized so that they could read them on the anniversary of their date written.

"Oh, you can't read that without us. How will we know if they end up together?" Henry kids her. The Colonel used to always say 'and we lived happily ever after'.

Joshua, walks into the kitchen. "My bride would want to hear them also. She snuck a few peeks at them when she discovered them. Juliet Helen is very curious since she was named for the Colonel's wife, her great-great aunt Julia. I think it's cute that she prefers to be called Helen."

Carolyn says, "I heard you both get up very early this morn. Everything alright?"

He answers, "Helen was a little sick at about five this morning but has since gone back to bed. She isn't a morning person like the rest of us, anyway."

Anna hurries back into the kitchen and says, "I just told my folks that we are heading home to see them." She bends down to Clara Beth. "We are going to see Gramma and Grampa. Come on, we have to go back to the little house and get some things." She stands up with Clara on her hip. "I want to take advantage of the day, while it is still early." She reaches out for Henry's hand, "Come, Henry." She gives Carolyn a smile. "Thanks for the day off, sister. It is just what I needed." With that, she, Henry and the little girl are out the back door, in Henry's truck and headed down the road to the little house.

Carolyn looks at Joshua who is suddenly very serious looking. "What's wrong, little brother, is Helen seriously ill?"

"I don't know, sis, Helen is not happy here, I think. She was crying in her pillow, last night. I tried to comfort her and ask what was making her sad and she just shrugged my hand off her back. She isn't telling me anything. I know she is young, but she wanted to be married more than I did. I think she is regretting her decision."

"Oh, Joshua, I am so sorry. Being married is work. I had a hard time the first month or two. Being his Missus made me feel like I had lost my identity. It's not easy to explain. I went from running my own business to being Mrs. Eddie James. I wasn't *me* anymore." She heads over to the coffee pot, and feels it. It is cold, so she shrugs her shoulders and turns to Joshua. "Do you want me to talk with her?"

"I don't know if she will talk to you if she won't talk to me. I don't want her unhappy. I love her, Carolyn. I don't want her identity. I want her by my side in everything."

"Don't tell me, tell Helen."

"Tell Helen what, Carolyn?" Helen is standing in the

7

kitchen doorway, still in her gown and robe and barefooted. Her normally beautiful short wavy blonde bob is uncombed. She looks to her husband of eight months. "Joshua, are you talking about *us*? This is one of the things that upsets me. We have no privacy at all. You had to ask Carolyn if we could have the master suite. Now, you are telling her our private stuff? Is Anna in on this, also? Where is she?" She looks around the kitchen.

Joshua puts his hand out to take her arm, but she pulls away from him, as he says, "Anna is on her way to EL Dorado for the day. Helen, it was only right to discuss the room with Carolyn. It was our Grandparent's room, and she had to be as ready to turn it over as I was. I love you, Helen. I don't know what to do for you. I know you are not happy and I need help. How can I help you be my bright and shining bride, again?" She has turned her back on him. She is very demure, only five foot two so Joshua being a foot taller than she, towers over her. He is right behind her, afraid to touch her but he feels he must. He puts his hands on her shoulders, and she lets him turn her around. "How, Helen, tell me how? You know I love you. I would do anything for you. What do you want?"

He looks in her eyes. She has tears in them to match his. "Joshua, I love you, too." She wavers. "I think I am just homesick. Can I just go home? I can hitch a ride with Anna. I want to stay a few days, Joshua. Talk with my father, see some of my friends. You can come out for me on Sunday. It's only a few days. Can I go?" She pleads.

"You want to leave me? You think that will solve anything? You're my wife. I want you here. I *need* you here."

Carolyn feels trapped, being a witness to what should be a private conversation. She turns back to the stove and turns on the burner, then changes her mind and quietly moves toward the doorway.

Helen sees her move. "Carolyn, I can leave, right? I have your permission?"

This stops Carolyn in her tracks. She turns around. "*Permission?* Why do you think you need *my* permission? I am your sister-in-law, not your warden. You had no brothers or sisters, Helen. You don't seem to understand how siblings work. We are best friends, and we are family. We live in the house together, and make decisions together. I am not his boss or yours, and Joshua isn't the boss, either. He is your husband and he loves you. He doesn't want to be separated from you, but no one can and no one will stop you if you want to leave. I will call Anna at the little house and ask her to wait for you if you want, or you can take my car. But in my opinion, you need to work this out and going a hundred and forty miles away isn't going to help."

Helen juts out her small chin. "I asked for your permission, not your opinion. I will take your car, though, since you offered it." She brushes past Carolyn and heads to the doorway. "I am going to pack, Joshua. Come upstairs so we can talk, *alone*, while I do it."

Carolyn goes to stop her. "Why am I the enemy? I have done nothing but try to be a sister to you. Tell me, what I have done to wrong you?"

Helen keeps walking without answering Carolyn's questions. As Joshua goes by, he stops to puts his hand on her shoulder, then bends down and gives her a kiss on the forehead. "Let me try to talk with her. This separation might help, but I have the sick feeling that we are headed for disaster," he says as he shakes his head and follows Helen up the stairs.

Carolyn is left speechless. She thought that Helen was too young at seventeen to be wed, but she did not voice those thoughts. Joshua and Helen had a whirlwind romance, in Carolyn's opinion. She and Eddie dated for a year before he asked for her hand. Helen and Joshua dated only six months and it was all long distance. They talked on the phone more than looked in each other's eyes. Helen loved the fact that Joshua was older and was running his family plantation just like her father, Grant Johnson III, had at the age of twenty-four. Helen had seemed to love everything about Joshua, the Colonel and Legacy Plantation. *What went wrong in just eight short months?* She sighs.

She has a sudden urge to talk with Eddie. She looks at her

9

watch. It is only ten in the morning. Eddie is teaching class at the University of Kansas in Lawrence. When she met him, he was a Professor at Washburn University in Topeka, but when he decided to ask her to marry him, he transferred to the college closest to Carolyn. *He* didn't mind living on the Plantation and being part of a larger household, and he was an only child also. They just celebrated their first anniversary. Eddie fit right in with the family. He never had a problem with all the activity of their farm. Of course, he has his own career. *Maybe, Helen needs a career, or needs to go to college. Maybe she just needs to have a purpose,* Carolyn is thinking.

She walks to the stove and turns the burner on under the coffee. This afternoon, she has an appointment at the Farm Bureau office for a presentation of her newest bug sprayer. She has everything set up for it, and just needs to get her courage up. Speaking in front of people is the *only* thing that Carolyn, the normally take charge lady, fears.

When she has her hot coffee in her cup in front of her, Joshua comes down the stairs with a few bags. *It looks like Helen is staying for more than just a few days,* she thinks. Carolyn leaves her cup and goes to her brother who looks like he is holding back tears. "She is really doing this? How long is she staying away?"

Before Joshua can answer, Helen is coming down the stairs herself. "I am not sure how long, Carolyn. I am taking *OUR* car to EL Dorado so I will not need yours, but thank you for the offer." She walks out the front doors without turning around or saying good-bye. Joshua picks the cases back up and follows her out. He puts the cases in the back seat of the 1938 Buick Century Sedan. He opens the driver's door for her and attempts to hug her good-bye. She gives him a kiss on his cheek but does not hug him back. As soon as she is in the seat, she turns the key and drives off without hesitation.

Joshua comes back into the house with his head down. Carolyn goes to him, "I am sorry, Joshua. Is there anything I can do?" He shakes his head no. "Did she say what is going on or why she is upset . . . with me? Is it our closeness? How can she . . . how can we? . . . What can we do?"

"I gave her with a little gift for our anniversary. We met two years ago, today." He sighs, again. "She didn't say thank-you. Instead she said she needs time. She says that she wants us to be by ourselves. I told her that I don't intend to leave my family home. Then she said that it is only fair since she had to leave hers. Her family has had that home for seven generations. She was the last Johnson born in that house, and if she has given up her family home for me, then I should give up my family home for her. I understand her point. I should match her sacrifice. I just never thought that I would have to leave my home to keep my wife." He goes into the front parlor and sits on a chair with his head in his hands. "I have to figure some things out."

Carolyn goes to his chair and kneels next to it. "You should stay in the house. I should be the one who leaves. Eddie wouldn't mind us to have our own house. Now that I am getting more business with my inventions, and I do less for the farm, it makes more sense for me to go on my own."

"I don't know if that will be enough for Helen. There is still Anna, Henry, Frank and baby Clara. She feels threatened by their presence also. She is insecure, I think. She doesn't even know that I was interested in Anna while she was Rosanne. You were right about my feelings for Anna back then; she is our long-lost sister that has found her way home. What I felt toward Anna compared to what I feel about Helen is no . . . um." He gives up trying to find the right word. "comparison." He sighs, "It is eating me up alive that I am not enough for Helen. All I know, is that I just have to get through this next week." He says without any hope in his voice.

"Why don't I call Susan and ask her to talk with Helen? She can make sure she's arrived safely, and she might be able to see what is making Helen so unhappy. Helen has always thought of Susan as sort of a big sister, since she is an older cousin. Cheer up, brother, all is not lost. Helen says she still loves you. Just keep that as your hope." She ruffs up his hair. "Don't you have some last paychecks to write so the employees can start their winter hiatus? Keep busy. It will take your mind off your troubles for now. Okay?"

"Yes, I will go to work. Did you want me to go with you to the Farm Bureau? I can help you demonstrate the sprayer. It will keep me busy, as you say."

"That is a generous offer, Joshua. I'd appreciate the help. You know I do not like talking in public like this. I need to leave here by one. If you get those checks written quickly, we can go to a café downtown beforehand, especially since we don't have Anna here to serve us lunch, and we need to eat."

"And who's fault is that?" Joshua stands up. "Giving the help a day off, just 'cuz'!" He walks past her and gives her a loving punch in the jaw as he leaves out the kitchen back door to go to the farm office.

TWO

October 31st, 1939
Tuesday In EL Dorado, Kansas

When Anna and Henry arrive at her sister Melinda's home, her mom, Judy Masters has a large luncheon buffet all prepared. Anna's parents live with Melinda and Mark in their four-bedroom home. Anna's brother Matthew, his wife Susan, and their one-year old, Kathryn Ann were there waiting, also. Melinda was still working at Petro's Kroger Grocery. She will be off shortly, at three o'clock.

Melinda is working shorter hours because she is going to have their first baby. Petro and Joan, the Greek couple who run the store will not allow her to work more than 6 hours even though she is only in her fifth month and has had no trouble with morning sickness or the heavy fatigue that often accompanies a 'bun in the oven'.

Judd and his wife Judy run out to meet Henry's truck which carries the couple, their two-year-old and Henry's father, Frank. Da, as Henry calls him, is a childhood friend of Judd and Judy's. Both the Harrick's and the Master's had small wheat farms in Hope, Kansas but the over farming of wheat drove the price down, and then the Depression hit along with an eight-year drought. One magazine called it the Dustbowl Era because of the horrific, sometimes constant dust storms. Both men lost their farms to the bank, and moved away and became migrant pickers to sustain their families. They spent four years apart before accidentally meeting up at the Johnson Family Farms tomato field encampment in 1935.

After everyone hugs hello, Judy claims little Clara Beth. "Come to Gramma, Clara. I have some special treats just for you! My, have you grown since I saw you two weeks ago!" The Masters and Harrick family meet twice a month for Sunday dinner, sometimes at Legacy Plantation in Lawrence, sometimes here in EL Dorado.

Once inside the home, the family settles down to a feast.

Judy is a wonderful cook, something she passed down to Anna but not to her younger daughter, Melinda. Not that she can't cook, it's just that, well, she is better with numbers than a cookpot. Mark, himself, is a decent cook (he lived alone for years) and is in the kitchen helping Judy more than Melinda.

Anna has her niece, Kathryn Ann, on her lap. Katie Ann, as they call her has not started walking yet, but can stand up while holding on for ages. "Her balance and leg strength is all there. She just doesn't know it yet. I was in no hurry for Clara to walk, I knew I would do nothing but chase her once she did." Clara looks up from her small plate of food when she hears her name, and smiles. Judy was feeding her instead of letting her eat by herself. "Ma, she can eat the finger food herself. Eat your lunch, while it is still warm!" To prove her mother right, Clara picks up one of the pieces of chicken that Judy has already cut for her and shows it to Judy and her mother then puts it in her mouth with an exaggerated motion. Everyone watching, laughs.

Susan puts her hand on Anna's arm. "So how is my cousin Helen getting along? Carolyn called me and asked me to talk with her. What has Helen so upset about that she needed to come back home to EL Dorado?"

Anna looks at her strangely. "What do you mean? She was home in bed, when we left the plantation. Did something happen?"

"I was hoping you can tell me. Carolyn just asked if I could call on her at the Johnson Family farmhouse, tomorrow, and see how she is. Seems like an odd request but I am too curious now, not to call on her. I hope everything is alright."

"I am very curious, now, myself. We would have waited for her. Did she drive here by herself?" Anna asks. "I have never driven it by myself. Though, she is a more modern girl than I ever was."

The little girl standing on her lap decides to sit down with a plop, and takes Anna by surprise. "Katie Ann, you gave me a start!" She bends down and gives the little blonde a kiss on the forehead. "Matthew, how did you manage to have a such a light skinned little blondie?" She calls to her brother, who has an olive complexion with light blue eyes and dark hair.

"She is the spitting image of her beautiful mommy, isn't she?" Matthew looks around. "I followed your lead, Anna. You didn't let Henry contribute anything to Clara's good looks, she is all you!" He is next to Henry, and gives him an elbow in the ribs.

Henry takes the bait, "Brother, she may have her mom's beauty but she has my heart! It is wrapped around her little finger. It amazes me, how much you can love your child. Why didn't anyone teach us this in school? I know, I wasn't at all prepared."

Henry's Da, Frank, butts in, "I think I mentioned it a time or two that you became my pride and joy the moment you were born and bawling your eyes out! Did you think I was joking?"

Judd offers. "You do like to joke, Frank. Who could ever take you seriously?"

Frank responds with, "Well, I never!" Which makes everyone laugh.

Henry looks to Judd. "So are all the crops to market and the farm put to bed? We just need to till a few acres in and we are done. The last of our seasonal workers are gone."

"Yes, we are done with all the harvests. Grant has been very busy and we have not had a chance to talk with him about next year's crop rotation. I have put a few calls to him, but he hasn't returned them. Matthew and I have everything projected, and ready to order the seed, we just need his sign off. Has Carolyn come up with anything new in the last month or two?" Judd is always fascinated with her farm saving inventions.

"She is taking her smaller size bug sprayer to the farm bureau today to debut it. *She* was very nervous about it." Henry says with great emphasis that makes them chuckle, because she is so confident about *everything* else!

Melinda bursts into the house. "What is going on? Why are you here in the middle of the week?" She looks at her family. "Is there anything wrong?"

Anna hands Katie Ann to her Mommy, and crosses the room to hug her little sister. "We just came for the day. It's the

Colonel's birthday and I was moping around the house, missing him. Carolyn gave us the day off, so we jumped into the truck and came. How are you feeling? Let me look at you. Look how big you are getting!. Are you feeling good so far?"

"Well, I was until I saw Henry's truck and had a miniature heart attack!" She looks to her husband, father, and mother. "One of you should have called Joan to let me know."

They all look at each other, and speak at once. "I thought you called her." "Didn't you call her?" "I didn't think about it." Then they all shrug their shoulders and laugh. "Jinx, triple Jinx." The three of them now say in unison.

After the babies take their naps, Susan changes Katie Ann, while Anna tries to coax Clara to go in the big toilet. She says, "Clara, is a big girl, Auntie Susan. Do you want to see her make water in the potty?"

Susan plays along. "Clara, are you that big, already? Let me see you go, please?"

Anna puts her on the toilet and within a few seconds a small tinkle hits the water and Clara exclaims, "I go pee-pee in potty. I am big girl!" Anna is so proud. She gets her wiped and her hands washed and Clara runs into the living room and jumps on her father's lap. "I go pee-pee, Da-Da! In the potty!"

Henry hugs his little girl. "That's my girl, you are getting sooooo biggg!" He gives her a kiss on the forehead and it is enough. She squirms out of his lap to run to her Gramma to make the announcement all over, again.

The afternoon is soon at an end and Anna and Henry say good-by to all their relatives and start their long journey home.

THREE

November 1ˢᵗ, 1939
Wednesday in EL Dorado, Kansas

Susan is on the line, calling Helen at her father's house. Matilda, the longtime household maid, answers the phone. "The Grant Johnson Household, Matilda speaking, how can I help you?"

Her formal telephone greeting always tempts Susan to chuckle. "How are you Matilda? This is cousin Susan Masters, is Helen available?"

Now the true personality of the maid comes out. "Oh, Missus Susan! How iz you, chile? How iz that beautiful blondie Katie Ann? Pretty, as her mama still, I bet! When iz you coming to the Johnson House with that youngin'?"

"That is what I was calling Helen to find out. I understand that she is home and I thought that I would visit. May I speak with her?"

"Oh, forgive, ole Matilda, I'ze gets so excited 'bout babies, you know. I will go fetch Missus Helen, right away, now. Hold on." She puts the phone down and Susan is on the line for some time when a phone is picked-up in another part of the house.

"Hello? Susan? I am so glad you called. Hang on a bit." Helen covers the receiver and calls out, "Mattie, go hang up the line downstairs, I am on it up here." She takes her hand from the receiver, "Hold on a bit, Susan, I want to hear Mattie hang up first." They wait for a few seconds.

"Here you go, Missus Helen, I am hanging the line. Hope to see you soon, Missus Susan!" Matilda says and then line clicks.

"I know she listens in on my calls, she is so annoying sometimes. How are you Susan? How did you know I was home?"

Susan anticipated the question and said, "Matthew was talking to Henry, this morning. He mentioned it. Are you

17

staying long? Can we get together? Would you like to come see Katie Ann and have a little visit? It feels like we haven't had any time alone together since before I had Katie" She rushes out her practiced words.

"I do need to talk with my dear cousin, away from this house and Legacy Plantation. Can I come over around two, this afternoon? Will Matthew be home? If so, maybe you and I could go for a little shopping trip without Katie and talk." Her voice sounded strained, even to herself.

"Two would be lovely. Matthew isn't due back from classes until five or so. We would be alone, except for my baby girl, but Katie won't tell a soul what we are talking about. I promise." Susan is trying to keep it light. "Tell Matilda, I will bring Katie Ann there, real soon, though."

"Perfect, I will see you then, cousin." Helen hangs up and goes downstairs to see her father. He is in his study on the main level.

"Papa? Can I bother you?" She sees he is leaning over his desk with his head in both hands. "Papa, are you not feeling well?" She is at his side in an instant. He looks up at her and she sees his eyes look pained.

"Juliet Helen, not to worry. I am just tired and I think I dozed off. What can I do for you, my girl?" He runs his hands through his perfectly trimmed curly blonde hair. "I heard the phone, was that for you?"

"Yes, Papa, I am going to see Susan, this afternoon at two. It's cold in here. Let me call Sullivan so he can start a fire for you." She goes to the servant's rope and gives it a pull.

Grant Johnson stands and goes to his petite fair haired, daughter. "You needn't have bothered Sullivan. I am not cold. Daughter, I am worried about you. It is not natural for a newlywed to take little trips without her husband. What is going on with you? Aren't you happy?"

Before Helen can answer, Sullivan hurries into the room, "Sir, you rang?" He is a tall black man with gray at his temples. He and his mother Matilda were both born on the farm and have been employed by the Johnson family their whole lives.

"Thank you, Sullivan. It is getting chilly in here and my Juliet Helen feels a fire is in order, if you please." He puts his arm around his only child and leads her to the sofa on the other side of his study. "Is there anything that you'd like to tell me?" He asks, simply.

She watches Sullivan check the hearth and load the logs onto the grate. Grant is watching her watch him, knowing that Helen never liked talking in front of the servants. When the fire is going, Sullivan nods to his boss and hurriedly leaves the room. But, as Helen was about to finally say something, her Great-Grandmother Carolyn comes into the study.

"Oh, good, I am glad to catch the both of you. I wanted to let you know that I will not be home for dinner. I have a board meeting down at the Hospital but I am joining with a friend for dinner before we go to the meeting together."

Carolyn Lewis Johnson is seventy-four but has a social life of someone half her age. Widowed for twenty-nine years now, she enjoys the company of her gentlemen callers as well as her women friends. Her hair's brilliant red color has faded to a strawberry blonde and has white at the temples. She keeps it in the Gibson girl style of her youth. "Helen, if you are still in town on Thursday night, would you be interested in accompanying me to the EL Dorado Theatre? My friend, Mrs. Roosevelt, has sudden out of town guests and I have her ticket. You and I haven't been out together, since we went to my brother's birthday party where you met your Joshua. Be a dear and say you will come with me?"

"Yes, Grand Mamá, I think I will still be in town and I would be happy to be your 'date'."

"Good, that's settled. I am off, tootle-loo!"

Finally, alone. Helen looks up at her father. "Papa, I don't think I am happy being married. I feel that I don't have a say in any of the dealings of the household or the business. I thought I would have a bigger role in Joshua's life. His sister is the one he confers with about everything. What am I to do?" She lays her head on his shoulder as they sit side by side.

"Have you talked with him and explained how you feel?" When he feels her shrug against his shoulder, he sighs. "You need to talk this over with him. He is a bright young man who truly loves you, Helen. You just need to communicate with him."

"I don't want to hurt him. You should have seen the look in his eyes when I said I wanted to come home. I know he loves me, Papa and I love him but I don't know how I can tell him that I need more."

"Your Mama, God rest her soul, needed more, also. She didn't want to run the farm with me so she volunteered all around. When that didn't work, then she took up her music lessons again. Soon afterward, I bought her that baby grand, and she found her place. Do you remember her playing? She was so gifted and soon we had lots of children coming here for lessons. She was finally, happy. It's a shame that she isn't here for you, Helen. She would tell you to find something to do that you can love. Like she loved her music."

"I remember all those children in our house. I used to get jealous because she spent time with them and not me, except when she taught Susan. I loved having Susan over to play with me before and after her lessons. I even enjoyed watching them play beautiful music together. If you recall, I had no natural inclination toward music so Momma and I didn't have that to share. Then she died so suddenly." She pauses, then continues. "Papa, how did you stand it? I would die, if something were to happen to Joshua."

"I had to go on, Helen, I had you. You were the reason that I got up each morning. You still are, my girl. Even though, we live so far from each other, you are in my heart always." His arm around her tightens into a squeeze. "Now, go get ready for your outing with Susan. And do not fret, little one. You will figure this out, I promise." He lets go of her, stands and holds out his hands. "Come on, off you go. I have work to do and I cannot do it with you leaning on my shoulder. You are a grown woman. Stand tall and get moving."

Helen reluctantly leaves her father's study. His words of comfort helped. *If only he knew the other reason I am so unhappy!* She gave herself a little shake to push the other thoughts from her mind. She ran up the stairs and changed clothes for her afternoon with Susan.

***

Susan had just come in from the market, where she picked up a few sweet cakes to serve Helen. They had become even closer during the time she began dating Joshua. Being the older married cousin, Susan gave Helen a safe place to 'ooh' and 'ah' over everything Joshua did or said. Susan had no question that Helen was truly in love with him. *That is as obvious as the sun in the sky. So, what is happening, now?* She wondered.

As is typical of Helen, she arrives five minutes early with a curtesy knock-knock on the front door. "Susan, it's me," she announces as she enters. The three-bedroom home is a small bungalow on Washington Avenue. Susan's mother and grandparents gave the home to the couple as a wedding gift. It is walking distance to Susan's part-time job at the EL Dorado Public Library. The home that she grew up in was a few walking blocks in another direction. There is no answer to Helen's knock, so she calls out again. "Susan, it is Helen, I am here!"

Susan calls from the kitchen. "Helen, come here quick. Katie Ann is walking!" Helen runs to the large kitchen just in time to see the baby girl plop down on her butt, in the middle of the kitchen floor. "You missed it. Katie, do you want to show Helen you can walk?" She looks down at the baby who seemed perfectly content to sit awhile. "If only she had done this last night! We were at Melinda's with the whole family. Her first steps, I cannot believe it! She is younger than Clara Beth was, for walking."

"Oh, you are trying to outdo perfect Anna's baby? Good luck with that!" Helen says as she sits down at the kitchen table.

Ignoring that comment, Susan picks up Katie and puts her in a playpen filled with toys, and turns to Helen, "Tea or Coffee with your sweet cakes?"

"I will take tea, please, but no cakes. Matilda has been making me 10-course breakfasts and lunches! She is fussing over me like an old mother hen. I can hardly breathe!"

"She raised you, Helen, what do you expect? It is the same when I go to my Grandparent's home. Dee-Dee fusses over me and the baby as if she hasn't seen us in months, instead of days. Not that I would have it any other way. My family can act a little stoic, most of the time. Not a feeling ever shows across their faces. I know I must take after my father's side because I can hardly keep my face from telling all." While she is saying this, she is busy pouring out the hot tea. "You too, Helen, every feeling shows on your face. Now, do you want to talk?" She pours herself a cup and sits.

Helen is sipping her tea, weighing her words, carefully. Even though Susan is Helen's cousin, Susan has known the Lewis family for three years and has been devoted to the Masters Clan for the last four years. *Can I honestly tell her?* "This tea is wonderful. The Lewis household are avid coffee drinkers, especially Carolyn. The Colonel was the only tea drinker in the house. I do miss him. He was a sweet old man."

"If you asked Anna, she would make sure a fresh brewed pot was always available for you." Susan said, trying not to sound defensive of Anna.

"I'm sure . . ." Helen trails off, then becomes silent.

Susan knows that she cannot press her. "Helen, after tea would you like to go shopping? We would have to take Katie but she is very good in a stroller. We can window shop downtown, if you like. Nothing picks me up when I have the blues more than a brand-new hat. Shall we find you a new one?" She sees a hint of a smile on her cousin.

"That would be very nice, Susan. Let's do that. I haven't shopped downtown in ages."

They spend a couple of wonderful hours going from Haberlein's to Kittie Clarks to Famous Clothiers to Scott's Ladies Wear and even went into the J.C. Penney store. Helen was amazed at the quality for the low price of things.

"I know that this is Anna and Henry's favorite store, but they go to the one in Lawrence. I must admit, I have never been in here. Matilda always said that the store was for 'poor white trash'. I think she is mistaken." Helen and Susan both laugh. Helen has purchased quite a few things and they get to the bungalow just as Matthew comes home laden with books.

"Wow, did you ladies leave any merchandise for other shoppers?" He says as he helps unload Susan's few items. The back seat was still filled with packages. "Did you ladies have a good time, then?"

"The best!" They answered together. Susan looks at her to say "Jinx . . ." but she can see that Helen is not fond of the Masters private joke. Helen says her good-byes and leaves so she can join her Papa for dinner, which is always at six sharp.

After she is gone, Matthew asks, "Did you find out what's the problem?"

Susan shakes her head. "She seemed close to sharing a few times, but she never did. She is wrapped up tighter than a newborn in a swaddling blanket! She is hurting I can see it, but she just cannot let it out. I get the feeling that it has something to do with Anna and Carolyn's presence in the household. Not that she said anything, exactly. She has a bit of resentment that came out few times. When she slipped, she tried to cover it up. I have no advice to give Joshua. That makes me sad for them, both!"

FOUR

November 2nd, 1939
Thursday in Lawrence, Kansas

Joshua is in the upstairs hallway on the phone. Anna can hear him all the way in the kitchen. "Mattie, please help me here. I haven't talked to her since she went home. I am getting sick with worry." Then came silence on his end.

"She went with her Grand Mamá Carolyn? No, that makes me feel better. Is Mr. Johnson available? Can I speak with him?" His end was quiet a second time.

"Good evening, Grant. How are you feeling?" Pause. "Sir, I was wondering if you can help. You know that I love your daughter very much. Is there any advice that you can give me to win her back? She hasn't taken my calls. Matilda says she is out, each time but she hasn't called me back, either. I am at my wit's end."

Anna can hear desperation in his voice. She hates that Joshua is going through this so soon in the marriage. He is such a good man. Funny, handsome and considerate. He deserves a wife that idolizes him. She wanted that for him, even back when she was Rosanne. She loved him as an adopted brother but knew even then that she wasn't that person. This second rejection for him is just unfair.

She has the dinner dishes finished and everything put away. She goes into the sitting room, where Carolyn is reading and Eddie is working on his class' papers. "I am going to head home, now. Is there anything I can get for either of you before I leave?"

Carolyn puts down her book. "Tomorrow, we have to get those letters, and journals out. I think we need to take Joshua's mind off his missing wife." She crosses over to Anna and takes her out into the hallway, just at the base of the stairs. She listens for the continuation of the phone conversation upstairs. Hearing nothing, she says, "I feel so helpless and at the same time mad at Helen for putting him through this. I think distraction is the best way to deal with this. I think we need to start reading from the collection. Do you think that will be okay?" She has her hand on Anna's arm.

Anna puts her hand on Carolyn's. "I think that would be great. I have been anxiously waiting to read if the Colonel and his Julia end up, together. Aren't you curious?" She winks at her.

"Very funny! Your husband used that same kind of joke the other day. Good-night Anna. See you in the morning." They kiss each other's cheek and Anna turns to the back of the house to go out the kitchen door. Henry is waiting in the truck to take her home.

Carolyn goes back into the sitting room and picks up her book. She cannot concentrate on it. She sighs, loudly then says, "Eddie, do you like it here? We should start looking for our own place. I think Helen needs to be the Mistress of the Manor. We can move in a little place near downtown Lawrence or near the University. What do you think?"

Eddie puts his pen to the side of his face and taps his cheek in thought. "It doesn't matter where I lay my head. As long, as your head is next to mine. It would be nice closer to the University but I know you, Carolyn, you wouldn't like being away from the plantation, Joshua or Anna. I will follow you where you think you need to go but we will end up back here. I will have Matthew take book on it." He chuckles. "The last time Matthew was here, he mentioned taking a Criminology course. Professor Bailey has retired from teaching so he was asking me if I had heard of any of the remaining professors. I do not know where he'd like to go with this but he would be a great detective."

"Eddie, you've changed the subject." She throws a pillow at him. "I would like to seriously discuss this."

"I have nothing more to add on the subject. We can look, but I would hate to sign a lease then have you be here most of the time. I think you need to talk to Joshua about this."

At the doorway, Joshua asks, "Talk to me about what?" Carolyn can see he has been running his hands through his hair out of frustration.

"Anna and I want to read the letters from your bedroom. We've put them all in order. Do you want to start them tonight?"

"It's a little late, Carolyn. I will be turning in soon. I know that you wanted to start days, ago. But that was not what you were talking about before I came in the room. I heard the words 'move in'. Are you on that again?"

Eddie sings. "Car-O-lyn is cAU-ght!"

She ignores her husband's taunting. "I think that if your bride wants you to herself, we should respect that. Eddie doesn't mind moving. I could learn to be happy somewhere else."

Joshua looks her in the eye while a small smile begins to spread on his face. He walks to the couch and leans down over her and gives her a peck on the top of the head. "Liar, liar, pants on fire. We will start your letters, tomorrow after dinner. Eddie, keep your wife in line, could you?"

"I wouldn't dare! I know my place."

"I envy you, that."

"No word from Helen, then?" Carolyn asks since he mentions her in a round-about way.

"Tonight, she's out with your namesake, apparently. I talked with Grant but he said that Helen needs to make up her own mind, that he will not push her. I asked him to please see that she calls me in the morning and he said that he would. I will just have to sit on my hands and wait. He doesn't understand that I am going crazy just waiting."

FIVE

November 3rd, 1939
Friday in Lawrence, Kansas

Carolyn is on her third cup of coffee and they have the letters out. Clara Beth is playing on the floor with her toys. Weeks ago, when they organized them all, and they realized they are not just from the Colonel, Gram Julia, and Great-Gram Beth, but from Grant Johnson (the first) and his bride Carolyn as well as all the other siblings of the Colonel's. They have filled several shoe boxes, in an effort, to organize them.

Carolyn is very excited. "I cannot believe that we, practically, have the entire family history here. I should ask my Aunts and Uncles if they have any letters from the Colonel or Gram Julia, before we start reading."

"You won't be able to wait, Carolyn. Who do you think you are fooling!" Anna kids her. "We need to get all of this out of the way." She sees her little girl squirming. "I think Clara needs a change before I can start lunch."

Clara looks up at hearing her name. "Mama, I go pee-pee in potty, peas?" Anna smiles that she is asking to go, on her own. She rushes and grabs her little girl and disappears into the little bathroom, next to the laundry room.

Joshua and Henry come in from the farm office. Henry looks around the kitchen. "Wow, is this all of them? Anna said there were a lot." He looks around the room. "Where is Anna?"

Clara Beth calls out from the bathroom. "Da-Da! Da-Da, I go pee-pee!"

He smiles and goes to the bathroom door. "What? Clara is *such* a big girl!" Anna and he exchange a few words that Carolyn cannot make out from the kitchen. Clara comes running out of the room and her father calls to her. "Clara Beth, you need to wash your hands!! Come back to me, please." Clara obediently but slowly walks back to the bathroom. Anna passes her and pats her head as Henry warns, "Today, little girl!"

27

This made Clara increase her pace. "I a *big* girl, I go pee-pee on potty!" She says defiantly.

"Yes, but big girls always wash their hands." They can hear the water running, then it stops and Henry adds, "Now, *that's* a big girl." He brings her out of the bathroom. "Clara has clean hands after potty!" He announces. Everyone praises her at the same time. Clara beams and goes back to her toys.

Carolyn remarks, "You two are the best parents. It is so natural for you." She looks to Henry when he says this. "You were an only child. How do you know how to do this?"

"Little children are little problems. I cannot say if I will have the answers when she gets bigger." He shrugs. "I hate to rain on this parade but I am starving. What can I do to help, so we can eat?" He has his hands on one of the boxes. "Can I move these back to the day room?" He is referring to the small room on the other side of the kitchen that was a servant's room, when the house was first built. This was the room that Anna used to nurse Clara and where Clara now naps during the day.

Anna is waiting for Carolyn's decision. They have decided where to start reading and the rest are not necessary at this point. Also, Anna can't prepare a meal with so much clutter on the island. Carolyn gives consent to move them and they all begin the process.

While they are moving the boxes, Joshua's strained voice can be heard on the upstairs phone, again.

"Don't you think that I have been patient, enough? I want to talk with my wife!" After a few moments of silence, you hear Joshua slam down the receiver. Everyone in the kitchen freezes in place.

Henry whispers, "This isn't his first call to Helen, this morning." Carolyn and Anna nod as they continue.

Within a few minutes, Anna has grilled cheese sandwiches frying and a large salad made. Joshua can be heard going up and down the stairs. Carolyn goes to the hallway. "Lunch will be ready in just a moment, Joshua." She sees a small suitcase at the foot of the stairs. She waits until he comes back down. "Going to EL Dorado, then?" He nods and puts another small bag next to the first. They reenter the kitchen.

He explains. "I don't understand what is going on. I don't know if the household is against me on Helen's orders or Grant's. Are they keeping me away from her or is she behind this? If she doesn't want to be married to me anymore, then just tell me that. I will admit defeat. But I cannot go down without understanding what has happened! I need to know what I have done or if I can fix this. She was happy here as my bride and now suddenly, she isn't. Something happened and I have to get to the bottom of it before I can let her go." He looks around the room to Henry. "I know that you can understand. You lost Anna and refused to believe it. Right now, I feel like I am looking at that headlamp that made you realize something terrible happened to her!" He is referring to seeing Anna's father's truck at the home of her attacker that was used to run Anna down. They all nod, speechless.

Anna was at the stove with her back to them as he says this. She suddenly feels weak in her knees, picturing her Henry seeing her hair and blood on the truck's headlamp. She grabs onto the counter to steady herself. No one notices because they are focused on Joshua. The weakness lessens but she begins to shake at the thought of what her family went through, seeing the proof of what they were told, that she was murdered. A tear escapes her right eye as she regains most of her strength. She does the final flip of the sandwiches. "These are done," she announces weakly. She picks up the fry pan and turns around to plate the food. She is still feeling weak and the pan wobbles in her hand. Henry notices and reaches out for her. Joshua notices also.

"I am so sorry, Anna. That was insensitive of me. That was an awful time and I shouldn't have used it as a reference. I just feel as desperate as . . . well . . . as Henry, must have felt." He sits down at the island counter and cries out. "What if I lose her?" He breaks down in tears. "I can't . . . I just can't." He sobs.

SIX

November 3rd, 1939
Friday in EL Dorado, Kansas

Joshua ate Anna's late lunch and insisted that they start the letters without him. He would catch up when he returns with his wife. He leaves to spend an hour at the farm office before heading out to get his wife. The 140-mile drive is torment for him. His mind was going faster than his truck could drive. What is he going to do first? *Demand to see her, force my way in?* He is at a loss for a plan. Should he get Susan to get Helen for him? He hates to trick her into seeing him. He wants her to want to see him. He is picturing Helen slamming the door in his face. *What will I do, then?*

It is almost seven at night when he gets to the Johnson Estate farmhouse. This home is a mansion, even larger than their home at Legacy Plantation. If he forced his way in, he'd have a hell of a time trying to find her in a farmhouse such as this. Farmhouse is such an odd name for this beautiful home with eight bedrooms! His palms are sweaty as he rings the bell at the massive front door. Sullivan opens the door.

"Hello Sullivan, how are you this evening?" He tries to act casual and walk past him but Sullivan is blocking his entry with his large frame. "Excuse me, Sullivan, but I am here to talk with my wife, Helen."

"I am sorry Mr. Lewis. Missus Helen is not home." His large voice booms, and he still doesn't move.

"Well, let me talk with Grant Johnson, then." He tries again to get a foot in the door. "Please!"

"Let him through, Sullivan. We are not cavemen. Sorry, Joshua." Grant pushes Sullivan aside with little effort, considering that he is only five foot five and Sullivan is six foot six. "Come into the study for a moment. Helen isn't here, I am sure Sullivan told you." Grant leads Joshua through the entranceway down the hall. "Can I have him bring you a drink or some supper? It was a long drive from Lawrence."

"Water or cold tea would be nice, thank you." Joshua sits on the sofa as Grant goes back out to tell Sullivan to get them tea.

When he comes back in the room, he closes the door. "Joshua, I do not have anything else I can tell you. Helen has not told me anything, that I think would be a clue to help solve this situation. She has kept very busy, seeing old friends, and spending time with her Great-Grand Mamá."

"Where is she now, Grant?" Joshua is past being polite. He just wants to see her.

"I am not sure. She was here for dinner then afterward, I heard the car go down the driveway. She did not tell me she was leaving." Sullivan knocks lightly at the door and comes in without waiting for permission. He has a tray of drinks that he puts down on Grant's desk, turns, nods to Grant and leaves.

As the door closes, Joshua releases the breath he had been holding. "Grant, this is bullshit, pardon my language, but I want to see my wife. I will make myself at home until she comes home." He gets up and helps himself to one of the glasses of tea and takes a few sips. He is trying to simmer down with the cool liquid. He sits back down. "I am upset and I am sorry for the rudeness, but I am wit's end. I do not know if my marriage is over. Did I do something wrong? I love her, she loved me, I know it. Did she fall out of love? Does that happen in eight months? We've never fought, I have never raised my voice to her. No one has. I have given her everything she has wanted. WHAT DID I DO WRONG?"

"Joshua, I do not know if you did anything wrong. I do not know why she is unhappy, but she is. That is all I can tell you. I would not betray her confidence if she told me anything but she hasn't. I do not know where she is, and if I did, I would not feel right telling you that, either."

He pauses and crosses to the window and looks out for a moment. "I need you to leave, until Helen tells me that she wants to see you, I will not have you waiting to ambush her." He turns from the window, takes his tea and drinks several swallows. Then he goes to the servant's rope and pulls it. "I am going to have Sullivan show you out now. I will talk with

Helen when she comes home and *if* she wants to see you I will call you. Will you be going back to Lawrence? If not, where will you be staying?"

Joshua just looks at him, blankly. Sullivan comes into the room. "Sir?" He asks.

"Mr. Lewis is leaving, Sullivan, please show him out. Joshua? Where can I reach you?"

"I assumed I would be staying here. Can I not stay in a separate bedroom? Lock me in, until you have her permission to let me out if you must, but don't ask me to leave, PLEASE!"

"Out of the question. You cannot stay here. Sullivan, help Joshua off the sofa." Sullivan grabs his arm and with little effort brings Joshua to a standing position. "Don't make Sullivan get rough with you. Be a gentleman and leave, please Joshua. Go back to Lawrence. Or stay the night with Matthew Masters or Mark Collins. I or Juliet Helen will call you there, tomorrow"

Sullivan has hands on Joshua, again. Joshua is trying to free himself. "Why are you doing this, Grant? This makes no sense! This isn't fair. I am her husband! Grant! Grant!" He calls as he is being pushed out of the house.

When the front door is shut in his face, he screams, "Grant, I will make you pay for this. This isn't right! She's my wife! Let me in!!" Joshua starts banging on the door. "Grant, I will make you pay for this!!!" He continues this useless action for about twenty minutes. He feels like a fool. He knows he'd better leave before Grant calls the police on him. He just cannot believe he has been kicked out of the house for no apparent reason.

SEVEN

An excerpt from Elizabeth Lewis's Journal
Wednesday, November 3rd, 1880 - Lawrence, Kansas

Once again, I have put off the telling of my personal loss. It is so hard to resume life as it was before because nothing IS as it was before. I have been going through the motions for the good of the family but I am just a walking scarecrow. Or, I stand watching events that should bring happiness go by with no feeling.

I will try to tell my tale, and with it, I hope to relieve myself of the dullness that has replaced the color in my life. I miss color. I know it is still out there. I see everything as if it's a pencil drawing of the actual experience. I want to feel again!

I know that I suddenly stopped my journal writing some time ago. I was too raw at the time. Then as time marched on, my writing got farther away from me. I wasn't ready to explain the absence. Explain to whom, I wonder. I am not sure anyone will ever see this but I feel I owe it to my invisible audience to be honest, regarding the long spans of missing years. Now I must begin.

In early August of 1878, my son Ian, his wife Lydia and their eight-year-old son Joshua Nathaniel left with two hundred heads of cattle to drive and deliver them to the new outpost in Decatur County. The settlers there, had scraped together a large sum for the cattle purchase but insisted that the sum must include delivery. Ian wanted to experience a cattle drive, at least once. He was always challenging himself physically. He had lost his leg just above the knee in the Quantrill Massacre of 1863, here in Lawrence and taught himself to walk without a limp on his wooden leg. He made it a point to never let his lack of leg stop him from doing anything a normal two-legged man would do.

His wife Lydia, owned and managed the City Hotel after her father Nathan Stone was murdered in the massacre. She had just sold the property. It became too much for her, living on the farm with us and maintaining the hotel in the perfect fashion that she was known for. After giving birth to Joshua Nathaniel, she suffered several miscarriages and thought that stress had caused her inability to carry a child to term. Lydia insisted on going with Ian on this journey. Little Joshua told his best friend, Chilly, that he thought it would be the biggest adventure that anyone could have! Chilly is my youngest son, born Charles Palmer Lewis and who was few months older than his nephew Joshua Nathaniel.

It was with great sadness that I saw the little family off. They had built a cute little house for themselves on the property and I saw one or more of them every day. Ian was my William's right hand man and Lydia was a daughter to me in every way. Our two boys were thick as cold molasses. We had a good life.

Ian had picked the wrong time to travel to the newest county in Kansas. We didn't know that the Cheyenne Indians had left the Reservation in the Indian Territory near Fort Reno in Oklahoma. We didn't know that they were headed north to their ancestral homeland, where the hunting could provide food for their numbers. As they say, 'What you don't know can kill you.'

The Cheyenne were starving on the southern Reservation and thought that the 1500-mile walk would save their tribe.

If you are reading this, I did not write that number in error. It was 1-5-0-0 miles to the Northern Cheyenne Reservation in the Montana territory. Under the leadership of their two Chiefs, Dull Knife and Little Wolf, three hundred fifty-three Cheyenne - Braves, Squaws and their Papooses began their journey. They were young and old alike. By all accounts, they had but thirty horses among them that the braves rode to hunt, guard and guide them. The rest were afoot.

I must admit I hated the Cheyenne for what happened! I hated them as much as I hated William Quantrill for the massacre. I have read many newspaper articles and my son Will's letters regarding them and I do not hate them anymore, but pity them.

They were a proud but angry people. A desperate people in a desperate situation. If we only we had known.

EIGHT

November 3rd, 1939
Friday in EL Dorado cont'd

Joshua drives away from the Johnson place, madder than he has ever been in his life! He cannot think of what to do. *I won't go home without Helen,* he thinks. Joshua cannot believe that Grant thinks he could just walk away from his wife. He pulls over. *I need a drink!* The only one who would know where to get a drink in dry Kansas is Matthew. Joshua has heard about the craps and poker games that Matthew attends but he knows that they are not every night and not in the same location twice in a row. He heads to the nearest gas station, where there are always payphones in front. He just needs to call Matthew.

It is almost ten p.m. and no one calls at this hour, when the phone rang. Matthew cannot make much sense out of what Joshua is telling him. Susan cannot figure out who her husband is talking with. Matthew puts his hand over the receiver and tells her, "Joshua is in EL Dorado and fought with Grant over Helen. He is raving mad. I am going to go get him. I might take him to the game for a drink, is that okay?" Susan shrugs. Joshua has never been to their bungalow, so what else can Matthew do?

Matthew speaks into the phone. "Joshua, I will come get you. Which gas station are you at? Okay, yes, I know where you can get a drink. I will call Mark and we will come get you together, brother. Just wait there, we won't be long." He hangs up and turns to his wife. "This is bad. Have you talked with Helen?"

"No, not since her first day here when we went shopping. Was Helen home when Joshua fought with Grant?"

"I don't know, Joshua wasn't making sense. Expect us to have a house guest tonight. I will try not to be late or make too much noise when we get in. Have some blankets on the couch for him to bed down when we get in, okay?"

"Of course. I know it's late but let me call Helen and see what she knows. They were such a good couple to have disintegrated like this, so quickly!" She walks to the phone and dials the Johnson home.

It rings about ten times before Grant, himself, picks it up. "I told you not to call here! What do you want?" He yells into the phone.

"Uncle Grant? It's Susan. I am sorry for calling so late but I need to talk with Helen. May I, please?"

"Sorry Susan, I thought you were someone else." He says gruffly. "Helen isn't home, yet, and I do not know where she is or when she'll be back. I have to go, Susan, Good-night." He hangs up on her just like that.

Susan puts down the receiver. "Well, that was a waste of time. All I got was a 'not home, bye' from Grant."

"Do you want me to call Mark, before you get Joshua?" She has the phone in her hands, again, and is dialing her brother-in-law, before Matthew could answer. The phone is answered by Mark on the first ring. "Mark, Joshua is in town and in trouble. Can Matthew come get you to help with him?" She pauses. "He is on his way now, thanks Mark." She hangs up and goes to her husband. "Be careful, don't let him get drunk, I do not know if he has EVER had a drink before."

"Don't worry, my dear. I've got this." Matthew gives her a lingering kiss and is out the door.

It only takes Matthew seven minutes to drive to Mark's home. He is waiting outside. Once in the car, Mark says, "So fill me in, why is Joshua in town and what is the trouble?"

"Wife trouble. Helen has been home at Grant's all week and they will not let Joshua talk or see her. It sounds like it almost came to blows, tonight."

"Geez!" is all Mark had to say. "What is the plan, then?" Mark has always been direct and to the point.

"We need to pick up Joshua and bring his truck to my house. Then I thought we'd swing by Grant's and see if Joshua's car is on the property. If it's not, we will take him to a Poker game to get a drink, I think."

That is all Matthew has time to say, because they are in

front of the gas station and Joshua is standing outside his truck in his light jacket, shivering.

Mark jumps out of the passenger seat and says to Joshua. "Keys, please?" and holds out his hand for them.

Joshua says, "In the ignition, what are we going to do?"

Mark is already in the truck, but before he turns the key, he says, "Get in Matthew's car, he has a plan."

Joshua gets into Matthew's 1934 Ford Model 40. He notices that it is kept showroom clean. "You keep the car nice. Helen has most likely trashed my Chevy Sedan by now." He puts his head in his hands. "I feel like such a fool. I should have waited to marry her, she is too young to deal with a husband, and farm business. I thought she loved me! I need to hear her say she doesn't want me anymore. I cannot let this go!"

Matthew is pulling up to his bungalow and waits for Mark to park the truck and then he gets into the back seat of the car. Matthew starts out, again. "Joshua, did you see your car at Grant's when you were there?"

Joshua looks at Matthew. "The Sedan wasn't out in front but I did not look around the property. You mean she might have been home and hiding from me? I believed Grant when he said she had gone out."

"I think we should find out for ourselves. I know the back entrance that leads to the garage and barns. We will look around for your Sedan. If the car isn't there, then she isn't home, yet. We can either wait for her or go have a drink, like you wanted. Just one drink, mind you. Susan made me promise that I do not let you get drunk."

Joshua chuckles. "She is a smart lady."

"She is a very smart lady." Matthew reaffirms.

They ride in silence for a few minutes. Joshua is totally lost. He only knew the way to the front of the estate. He has never been on these roads. "God, I hope my car is here."

Matthew asks. "That brings up the question. What do you want to do if it is? I think the law is on your side that you have legal right to have custody of your wife. Grant has kidnapped her, essentially, from you. Do you know which room is hers from the outside?"

"Yes, I do."

"Well, I have played a few baseball games with Mark and I know he can throw very well. A few small rocks to her window will get her to look out, at least. That is my whole plan, so far. The rest we'll make up as we go. All in agreement?" He takes their silent nods as their yesses.

Matthew pulls onto a gravel road and turns off his headlamps. "We have to be very cautious from here." He warns. He drives very slowly and pulls up next to a small barn. "Look in here first." He reaches under his front seat and brings up a flashlight and hands it to Joshua. "The window is in front." Joshua slowly opens the front door, leaves it open and walks to the front of the barn. After a few seconds of shining the flashlight in the windows, he comes back to the car and gets back in.

"Not there. How many of these barns does he have? I know our property has eight such buildings. We can be here for a while."

"He has only three barns and a garage on the property. He has at least two barns on each farm he owns, but we won't be looking at any of them."

"It helps that you and Mark work for him. You know stuff, I don't, as just the son-in-law."

Mark says quietly in the back seat. "Yes, lucky us." Both Matthew and Joshua chuckle, despite the situation.

"We are at the biggest barn. Check it out. -- Mark, there should be another flashlight back there, you could look in the back windows while Joshua looks in the front." Both men exit the vehicle.

Moments later, they are both back in. "Not here." Joshua simply says.

"Well, the garage is our best chance, anyway. The last barn is not any bigger than a shed so I doubt your Sedan would fit in it anyway. Here we are." Both men get out again. They take a little longer than the last time. When they get back in, he looks at them, "Nothing?" He can tell the answer by their faces. "Okay, now we will check the side driveway from back to front. Then drinks are on you, Joshua." He tries to make light of the situation.

Within five minutes, they are on the way to the poker game. "Sorry, Joshua, but now we know that Grant was not lying about her not being home."

"Fine, but why not let me stay in one of the bedrooms so we can work things out? That is what doesn't make any sense." Joshua says with frustration. "Thanks guys for the ride, anyway. Too bad this wasn't under other circumstances."

The Craps/Poker Game parking lot was very crowded. Friday nights always draws the biggest players, because it is normally pay day for the working class. Since this was Joshua's first time at a game, he was in awe of all the activity and the fact that everyone knew Matthew and Mark, as well. Good to his word to Susan, they only have one drink, play just a little craps, socialize awhile then leave to go back home.

"Thank you for the distraction, Matthew. Henry always talked about you and these games but I see, he is not exaggerating! You are the one to beat. At least ten guys were disappointed that you were not playing tonight. How often do you come to these?"

"Three or four times a month. Between school, Johnson's Farms and my wife and daughter, I do not have much time. Though the games allow me to afford a few things that I have grown accustomed to." He waves to the vehicle.

After they drop off Mark, they head to the bungalow. Susan is asleep but she has left a pillow and blankets on the couch for Joshua.

"This is a nice place, Matthew. Thank you again for all that you've done tonight."

"Not a problem, Joshua. I just wish you were in the arms of your wife tonight instead of on my couch. But I am hopeful that you will hear from Helen, tomorrow. Do you need anything else?"

"No, I am good. I have a small suitcase in the truck, that I will go get. Thank you again, get some sleep. I am going to be fine out here."

Matthew walks up to him and holds out his arms. "You

are a good man, my brother. Things will work out." He says as he hugs Joshua. Then he turns and enters the bedroom.

Joshua sits on the couch for a few more moments. He looks at his watch. It is quarter to four in the morning. He is still trying to understand Grants actions. They are more baffling than Helen's. He sighs and with a slap to his knees, he is back up.

He needs his suitcase from his truck. He gets out the keys and lets himself out the front door. He opens the door of the truck and before he can reach in, someone hits him over the head with a heavy object that is dropped inside the truck front seat. Then the unconscious Joshua is lifted up onto the truck seat and pushed over to the passenger side. The keys are picked up off the ground. The truck is soon started and the attacker drives away with Joshua knocked out beside him.

NINE

November 4th, 1939
Saturday in EL Dorado

It was a little after six in the morning when the pounding on the bungalow door started. Matthew thought that maybe Joshua had locked himself out of the house but as he was on the way to let the persistent pounder in, he saw that the couch wasn't slept on.

The sheriff's police officers walked into the bungalow as soon as Matthew opens the door. "Are you Matthew Masters?" He asks impatiently.

"Yes, sir. I am. What is this about? Can I go put on some pants before we begin? I am not used to standing half naked at my front door."

"The shorts that you have on, will do fine for our line of questioning, at least for now."

Susan comes out of the bedroom, in a robe, holding Katie Ann on her hip. Katie is tired and puts her head on her mommy's shoulder. "Matthew, what is going on here?" She looks to the couch and, also, sees that the blanket and pillow for Joshua is exactly the way she left it.

Matthew says, "Okay, officers let's sit down at the table and start the questions. Can my beautiful bride make us some coffee? I could sure use it." Susan puts Katie in the playpen and goes into the kitchen and gets to work.

"Matthew, you own a 1934 Ford Model 40?"

"I do, sir. She is third on my list of things that I am proud of." Susan walks back into view and he winks at her.

"Well, Mr. Masters, your vehicle was seen last night on the Johnson Estate, do you want to explain why you were there?"

"Is that all? I was helping a friend look for his car. He had reason to believe it was on Grant Johnson's property."

"And why would Grant Johnson have your friend's car? He is one of the wealthiest farmers in Butler county."

"The car in question was driven by Grant's daughter Juliet

Helen Lewis. Her whereabouts were being withheld from her legal husband and I was assisting him to find his wife and his vehicle."

"Are you in Law school or something, kid?"

"Not yet, but I've hung out with enough lawyers, to sound convincing. Wouldn't you say?" He winks at Susan, again. She gives him a little weak smile back.

"What time was this, that you were on the property?"

"What time did your witness say he saw me?"

"Mr. Masters, I am the one asking the questions."

"Fine, we were there just a little after eleven. I suppose."

"And who is 'we'?"

"I was driving with Joshua Lewis, Grant's son-in-law, and my brother-in-law Mark Collins was also with us. Mark and I both work for Grant Johnson."

"Where is Mr. Lewis, now?"

Matthew points to the not-slept-on-couch. "He was right there when I said good-night to him. It was half past three in the morning."

"Are you sure about the time?"

"Quite sure, why? I don't think Grant would be making a big deal about our driving about the property. What is this all about?" Matthew says as he is holding out a coffee cup while Susan is filling it with piping hot coffee.

"Grant Johnson was killed at three in the morning. Joshua Lewis was heard threatening him earlier in the evening."

"*Grant is dead?*" Matthew and Susan both say together. Matthew puts his cup down.

Susan drops into a chair. "Oh, poor Helen, she'll be so lost without her father."

"Do you have any idea where Joshua Lewis is right now? We need to talk with him, as soon as possible."

"What about Helen and Uncle Grant's Grandmother, were they home? Did they hear or see anything? How about Matilda or Sullivan, they live and work at the farmhouse?" Susan asks worried.

"It happened just outside, in the woods next to the

property. He was shot. It woke up the household, who called the police. We found him dead."

Susan is on her feet. "I have to go to Helen, Matthew, you'll take care of Katie Ann?"

"Where is Helen Lewis, Mrs. Masters? She wasn't in the Farmhouse."

Susan sits back down. "I assumed she was at Grant's home, but Joshua was told that she wasn't home when he was there."

"And the car wasn't on the property at eleven, I wonder where she could be." Matthew says worriedly.

TEN

November 4th, 1939 cont'd
Saturday in Kansas

Helen now knows how foolish she has been! After dinner with her father, she decided to see an old friend from school on the outskirts of town. They had talked the day before and Kimberly was filling her in on her husband's job loss and his drinking. During their conversation, George came home and Kim hung up very quickly. Helen was worried about her and when she tried calling her earlier, George answered and said she was out. It just didn't seem, right. Helen felt that she needs to check on her. Ever since their talk, Helen was comparing George to Joshua in her mind and she knew that she had a good man and that she was being very silly worrying about not being as important to him as Carolyn and Anna were. She packed up her bags and loaded them in her car while her father was in his study.

She had dinner with her father and wanted to tell him that she was going back to Joshua but felt that he would try to talk her out of it. So, after dinner, she went upstairs for her purse and keys and she drove off without even a good-bye.

Kim answered her front door with an older nearly healed black eye, but a fresh cut split lip. She looked at Helen and said, loudly. "Tommy, I told you that I had no bottles to return, now scoot!" She swiftly shuts the door, and Helen could hear George yelling from the back of the house. She quickly went down the stairs and drove away. About two miles down the road, she stopped at a gas station and used the pay phone to call the police. She gave them Kim's address and told them that she was being beaten. She said that she didn't know who the man was but that it had been going on for a while by the bruises that she saw on the girl. They took her name and her information and asked if she would testify if anything comes of the investigation and Helen said, "Yes, absolutely! Just get the poor girl some help, please!" She was shaking when she hung up. She wanted Joshua's arms around her to protect her but she was three hours away from Legacy Plantation.

She drove to a small dinner that was on the edge of town and went in for a coffee. Hoping to calm her nerves enough to allow her to drive the long lonely road home.

When she reached Legacy Plantation, it was just after midnight. The house was dark. She grabbed just her one of her bags and let herself in the front door. She quietly went up to the Master suite and opened the door to find no one in their bed. *Where is Joshua? I need him.* The whole house was dark and quiet when she came in. He must be in his old room, she thought. She tiptoed to his room, and peeked in to see it was empty. She went back to the master suite, undressed and slipped into bed. *If he is tinkering somewhere in the house, surely he will come to bed, shortly.* She fell asleep with the lights on, waiting for him.

***

At seven in the morning, Eddie has made the coffee. He has an eight o'clock class to teach and Carolyn is having a cup with him. Anna comes in the kitchen of the main house just as Eddie is about to leave for class. She asks, "What time did Joshua and Helen get home last night?" The question, catches them both off guard.

"They are home? I didn't know." Carolyn says. She and Eddie exchange looks. He bends down and kisses his wife on the cheek. "I'll be home before noon." He leaves out the front door.

As Carolyn is standing at the door, watching her husband drive away, Anna says, "see Joshua's Sedan is parked out front, but not his truck." Carolyn makes a face. "No, it's not in the back, either." Anna answered as if she knew that is what the face meant.

Then the phone rings. The women look at the grandfather clock across from the staircase. "Who would call at this hour?" Carolyn says.

She and Anna go to the dining room to answer the phone. "Lewis residence, Carolyn speaking." She says by rote.

She listens for a second. "Slow down, Susan. I don't understand." Carolyn picks up the whole phone and puts it on the dining room table so that she can sit down on a dining room chair. "This is terrible. When did they say, it happened? I need to tell Helen. Yes, she is here. Well, the car she took to EL Dorado is here. I don't know about Joshua. He and Grant *what?*"

Suddenly, the doorbell rings. Anna answers it and it is two Douglas County Sheriff's Police. "We need to talk with Joshua and Helen Lewis, immediately!" The smaller one says. "Where are they, are they here?"

Carolyn says into the phone, "My God, the police are here!" and hangs up.

She rushes out of the dining room, in her usual take charge manner. "Officers, I am Carolyn James. I believe Helen is upstairs but I do not know where my brother Joshua is. Come this way." She leads them up to the room and knocks on the door. "Helen, open up. The Police are here to ask you some questions."

"Already? Wait, let me dress. It will only take me a minute." She says from behind the door.

The officers look at each other. *Was she expecting us?* "Mrs. Lewis, please come out now. You will have time to dress in a few moments."

She opens the door. "Is Kim okay? Did they find the man that was beating her?"

"No, Ma-am, we are here about your father." He looks to Carolyn. "Can we discuss this sitting down, in your front parlor, perhaps?" Carolyn silently, leads the way.

As they are all getting seated, Helen asks, "What is going on? What about my father?" She looks to Carolyn. "You know?"

"Susan called just before the Police came. I am so sorry."

She looks to the police. "What is she sorry about?"

"Mrs. Lewis, your father has been murdered."

Tears spring to her eyes. "Murdered? Who would want to kill my father?"

"Where were you last night around three in the morning?"

"Upstairs, asleep. I arrived home a little after midnight." She looks to Carolyn. "Where's Joshua?" She sobs.

Carolyn moves to sit next to her and puts her arms around her. "'Late yesterday afternoon, he went to EL Dorado to bring you home. Didn't you see him?"

"No, I didn't know he was there. I must have just missed him. I left my father's after dinner. OH!!! I didn't say good-bye to my father because I thought he would talk me out of returning to Joshua! *Oh, Papa. I didn't say good-bye!*" She repeats as she starts crying harder.

Anna goes to the bathroom for tissues and hands them to Helen and Carolyn who was crying with her.

The police look at the women. "None of you know where Joshua is?" They shake their head no.

"I have to go to EL Dorado. OH, my Great Grand Mamá, is she okay? They didn't hurt her, did they?"

"No ma-am, Mr. Johnson, was outside in the woods, they say, when it happened."

"How?" *Do I want to know?* "How did it happen?" She asks, hesitantly.

"He was shot, ma-am. I do not have any other details. Butler County police asked if we could escort you to them. If you would please go and get dressed now."

Helen stands up immediately and gets light headed and nauseous and sits back down. "I think I might be sick." She looks at Carolyn. "My baby will never know his Grandfather!!" and cries hard again on Carolyn's shoulder.

"You are pregnant, Helen? Oh, my poor sister, such happy news on such a sad day!" She strokes her hair. *This explains her behavior of the last few days,* Carolyn thinks, *sort of!*

Carolyn looks to Anna, "I will go with Helen. You man the fort here and call Susan immediately when Joshua comes home. Oh, and tell Eddie to call me at Grant's house. I should be there by the time he gets home."

"Come, sister. Let me help you dress." She takes her up the stairs. "We will figure this all out. Joshua will be so glad you came home. He loves you so much . . ." Her voice trails off as they walk into the bedroom and they shut the door."

ELEVEN

November 4th, 1939
Saturday in Butler County, Kansas

Joshua's head pounds. He reaches to the back of it and feels a lump the size of a chicken egg. He slowly opens his eyes. The daylight is blinding and is making his eyes tear. He looks at his watch: it is after nine in the morning. He is in his 1933 Ford Pick-Up truck. He is trying to remember why. He knew he was looking for Helen. The last thing he remembers, is being at Matthew's. *Wait, I was getting my grips from the truck!*

Suddenly a car horn blasts as a vehicle whizzes past. *What the?* Seconds later another horn and vehicle go past so close that the truck rocks from the displacement of air. He lifts himself off the seat to look out the window. *My truck is parked in the middle of the road!!*

He straightens up, and as his head continues to *thump – thump – thump*, he manages to get behind the wheel and reaches for the keys, but they are not in the ignition. He checks his pockets and looks on the floor and feels under the seat. His hand comes upon a piece of metal. He brings it out to see what it is. It is a gun - an old Navy Colt! He is holding it by the barrel. *I don't own this kind of a gun. How did it get here?* He puts it on the seat next to him and continues the search for the keys. Another vehicle speeds past him, but this one from the opposite direction. He turns to watch the car disappear behind him.

What is going on? Where am I? How did I get here? It is cold in the truck and the windshield has a light layer of frost on it. He must have been here for quite some time. He opens the door and steps on the running board. As he does so, his foot kicks the keys onto the road.

He is out of the truck and is bending down to pick them up when a County Sheriff's car pulls up behind him, with its lights flashing. *Oh, thank God, help has arrived!* "Officers, am I glad that you're here to help. I think I was attacked." He puts his hand on his lump, as if to show them. "I woke up here on this road. I don't know where I am or how I got here."

"Is this your vehicle?"

"Yes, as I as trying to tell you, something happened last night. I was staying with a family friend, and somehow ended up here."

The Officers look at each other. "Are you Joshua Lewis from Lawrence?"

"Yes, I am. Matthew must have noticed that I was missing. Look, I just found my keys, on the running board. Let me move my truck off the road and . . ."

The Officer next to him puts his arm on his shoulder to keep him from moving. The other officer is at the truck and lifts the Colt off the seat.

"I think I have found the murder weapon, Gordy. Keep your hands on him."

"Murder weapon? Who has been murdered?"

"Your father-in-law, Grant Johnson. You, Joshua Lewis are under arrest." He suddenly pushes Joshua around and has his face on the hood of the truck and he snaps the handcuffs on his wrists behind his back. "Billy, radio in that we have the suspect in custody and have them send a tow truck here for this vehicle."

***

Joshua is in the County Sheriff's office second-floor holding cell. He has not been told anything regarding the murder of his father-in-law. He has asked if his wife is safe. Was she home when it happened? *What about the other household members, the great-grandmother or the servants, were they unharmed?* His blinding headache is making it difficult to think through this insane situation. *I need to call Carolyn. Or should I call Matthew, since he is closer. Someone needs to come tell me if my wife is safe.* He yells to the room of Officers. "Please tell me if my wife is okay, that is all that I ask!" They look up at his outburst, but return to their work immediately. They have nothing to tell him.

***

The Douglas County Police drove Helen and Carolyn to the Butler County Sheriff's Office. Helen sobbed the whole ride, while Carolyn held her hand and let her lean on her shoulder. They were escorted to the Detective's Squad on the third floor. Once seated in the Investigator's office, Carolyn, thoroughly frustrated with the lack of information, starts pelting the Detective with questions before he has had a chance to take his seat. "What do you know so far? Do you have anyone in custody? Have you found my brother Joshua, yet? The Douglas Sheriffs had no information to give us. It's been three hours. You have to have clues to the killer by now." She rushes it all out with her pent-up energy from being cooped up during the trip.

"Let's start with introductions, first. I am Detective Maury Larkin. And you are?" He looks directly to Carolyn.

"I am Carolyn Lewis James, this is my sister, Juliet Helen Lewis." She reaches over to take her hand.

"Your sister? I was told that Juliet Helen Johnson was an only child?

"Officially, sister-in-law, but we don't do the 'in-law' game. Once you are married or 'adopted' we call each other sister or brother. I have an employee that is a sister in every way but blood." She sighs out loud with, "Ugh! Can you answer *any* of *my* questions, now?"

"I am sorry. Mrs. James, is it? Both of you are here to answer my questions." He turns his attention to Helen. "Mrs. Lewis, may I call you Juliet?"

She shakes her head no. "I, actually, prefer Helen."

"Okay, Helen. When was the last time you saw your father?"

She starts to tear again. "I had dinner with him at six sharp. I left for Lawrence, right afterward without saying good-bye to my father. I will regret that for the rest of my life, I never said good-bye!" She reaches in her purse for another handkerchief. They all seem thoroughly used. She doesn't take one out, but closes her purse back up and with an "Excuse me" gives a large sniff.   She looks back at the Detective.   "What else can I tell you?   I was home asleep in Lawrence when it supposedly happened."   She straightens her shoulders and juts out her chin.

"How long has this fight with your husband been going on with you in EL Dorado?"

"I came out on Tuesday.   Joshua and I have never fought. I was homesick and in a foul mood in Lawrence, I thought a few days in my father's house would cure that, and it did.   That is why I went home."

"You are very young, did your father approve of your marriage?"

"Papa loves Joshua."   She sighs.   "Oh my.   Love_d Joshua, I mean.   It will take a while to get used to the fact he is gone. Anyway, they got along great."

"Your husband was heard pounding on the front door of your childhood home, threatening your father.   Do you think he came back to kill him?"

"Never!!"   Carolyn and Helen answer at the same time. Helen continues, "Not in a million years.   He has trouble scheduling the cattle for slaughter."

"Yes, but he was very mad.   Your father would not tell him where you were and kicked him out of the house.   'I'll make you pay for this!' was what he was yelling."

Helen comes back at him. "Who heard him?   Matilda can barely hear the phone when it rings.   Grand Mamá had plans until after midnight, so she wasn't a witness, so that leaves just Sullivan who loves drama."

"It was the butler who said that he heard it.   But we found the gun that we think shot your father, it was in your husband's possession."

"You have Joshua?"   Carolyn interrupts.   "Why didn't you tell us?"   She is immediately on her feet.

Helen stands with her and interrupts, "I need to talk with him.   I need to tell him how silly I was for leaving Lawrence."

The Detective rolls his eyes.   "Didn't you hear me?   The murder weapon was found in his possession!"

Carolyn insists. "Detective, my brother is innocent and we will not cooperate with answering any other questions until *after* you have allowed his wife to see him."

Helen agrees, "Yes, no more questions until we see Joshua. I must insist." She says asserting herself in Carolyn's fashion. "Please?" She adds.

The Detective smiles at her. "If you insist, my dear. I will take you down there, myself." He stands up, "Ms. Carolyn, would you like to wait here, please. I will bring you down to see him, shortly.

Carolyn slowly sits back down. "Fine, as long as my *sister* sees her husband." She says with emphasis.

Helen looks at her and bends down to gives her a hug. "Thank you, sister." She says quickly and she exits out the door that the Detective is holding open. "Why didn't you tell me he was here? I have been so worried!" She says as they are walking down the stairs. She isn't expecting an answer.

Once on the second floor, the detective unlocks the hall door to the detention area. There are desks of working officers between Helen and the cell that is holding her husband. She sees him stand up when they enter.

"Joshua!" She yells to him.

"Helen?" He yells back.

"Thank God you are alright!" They both say at the same time. She crosses the room in ten steps. "Jinx!" She says with a weak smile. "Oh, Joshua, I am so sorry. I was being so silly! Are you alright?"

"Other than a killer headache." He starts to smile than realizes what he said. "Oh God, I am sorry, Helen. That was an awful choice of words. They told you about your father?" She puts her head down and nods. He continues, "I was mad at him for not letting me stay there and wait for you but after I left, I didn't see him again. I SWEAR, I didn't have anything to do with his death." He has tears in his eyes.

"Joshua, I believe you. You could never have done something like this. I don't understand why they think you did."

"Helen, I was at Matthew's and I went to my truck for my

grip and someone clobbered me and drove me and left me unconscious in the truck in the middle of the road. They left a Navy Colt under my seat which I found when I was looking for my keys to move my truck. The police found me and the gun before I was able to move the truck." He looks to the detective. "If I did this, why would I still have that gun? Why would I have a knot on the back of my head? Why would I park in the middle of the road to be caught?"

"I don't know but you did." He answered dryly. "Okay, Missus. I think that's enough."

"Wait! Joshua, did you say it was a Navy Colt?" She looks at the detective. "Papa has a pair of those in a box in his study. It has unusual markings on the handle. I would know it if I saw it. May I see it? I am sure that you'd like to know if it is his."

"Well, we compared it with the one still in the box so we are sure it is his. But thanks. I think that will do, Mrs. Lewis. It is time to go back upstairs to answer a few questions."

"What else can I tell you? I wasn't there. I do not know anyone that could to do this. I need to talk to my husband in private. Can we just have a moment alone?

Before the detective can answer, Joshua speaks up. "What is it, Helen?"

"Joshua, the reason I ran away . . ." She looks around. This is not the way she pictured telling her new husband that he is going to be a father.

The detective has his hand on her arm. "I think that is all. Now come with me little Missus." He pulls her away from her husband. "Back upstairs with you."

They spend another hour in the detective office, telling them nothing new. When they are allowed, to leave, Carolyn asks the officer, "May I see my brother, now?"

The detective shakes his head no. "Under the circumstances, I don't think that is a good idea."

"What circumstances? You promise me that I could visit."

"That was before you decided not to cooperate."

"We cannot give you answers we do not have!" Carolyn feels this is useless to plead. "At least can we get a ride to the

Johnson Estate? My husband should be there, by now."

"Fine, we can get you there. But stay in EL Dorado. I might have more questions for you."

Helen insists. "But we won't have any more answers. We've told you all we know! My husband is innocent!" Helen says, as she is shown out the door.

TWELVE

November 4th, 1939
Saturday in EL Dorado cont'd

Helen walks into her childhood home. She is emotionally drained from the stress. Together, Sullivan and his mother let them in and she asks about her Grand Mamá. "She is in her room. She has been abed since your father was . . ." Matilda cannot finish her sentence. "He was like my very own boy, he was." She begins to wail.

Sullivan takes her hand. "Maw, you mustn't take on so, we have our new Mistress to take care of." While Matilda wipes her eyes on her apron, Sullivan turns to Helen and Carolyn and says, "Mistress Helen, do you want to take your company in the parlor? Maw and I will get you some refreshments."

"No, Sullivan! I want to know what happened last night after I left!" She takes his hand and leads him to the parlor. "Sullivan, please sit and run it all by me. The Sheriffs would not tell us anything."

He sits down across from her. He shifts slightly in the chair as if uncomfortable sitting in this part of the house or maybe it is what he is about to say. "Well, Mistress – your husband came at seven p.m. and Master Grant had me show him out. He was awful mad! I ain't never seen nobody that mad!"

"Is that what you told the police?"

"Yes, Mistress, and I told them about Mr. Matthew's car on the property at eleven. They wuz looking in all the barns and sheds. Master Grant told me to retire after they left. I wuz sleeping in fits and starts, as it were, but Iz thought Iz heard or maybe I dreamt Master saying, 'I told you not to come back here!' I wuz finally asleep when Master Grant rang the study's servants bell. Iz hurried on my robe and went to see what he needed and the room was all turned over but he wasn't in it. Iz went to his bedroom next but he weren't there neither. Then I heardz yelling outside. I swore I heard Master say 'Stop, please for Juliet Helen's sake!' Then the gunshots rang out. I wuz awful scared, Missus. I iz so sorry! Your Grand Mamá came running down the stairs and saw the study and called the Police. Iz wanted to go help but Maw weren't gonna let me, no how. She held me back, she did! Screamin' hysterical like. Iz feelz so bad that I couldn't do nuthin' to save Master Grant!" He puts his head in his hands and sobs hard.

Helen gets up from her chair and goes to him. "Sullivan, it sounds as if there was nothing you could do. Look at me, Sullivan." She holds his large tear-streaked face in her hands. "Sullivan – it wasn't my Joshua – I swear – I know it wasn't him!"

"Iz don't know Mistress Helen; Iz know what Iz saw!"

"But you didn't see <u>him</u>, did you? Think about it!" Helen's face is red in anger. "Think about it," she repeats. "Did you see him after you put him out of the house?" She can tell he is considering it. He finally shakes his head, no. "I told you! You never saw him, did you?"

"No, Mistress. Iz didn't see no one after Mister Matthew's car left."

Matilda interrupts. "Sorry chile, he don't mean nothing against your husband. He is beside hizself with grief. You must be tired. Iz you hungry?"

Carolyn suddenly feels her stomach rumble. "Helen, we haven't had a bite all day. That's not a good thing for the child." She says that last part just above a whisper.

Though Matilda didn't hear the whispered comment, she begins to fuss. "Chile, I will go whip up a hearty lunch for you then. Go up and see your Grand Mamá. She suffers so. She has lost so many, the poor woman. Her husband so young, then all three of her babes, now her only grandson. No women should go through all this. It's just a pity . . ." She is padding off into the kitchen mumbling, now, to herself. "Iz, just not right." Sullivan silently follows her to the kitchen.

Helen collapses onto the sofa. "I cannot face Grand Mamá just yet. I need a . . . I don't know what I need, but . . ." She feels like she is going to cry, again. "I am done with these awful tears. They are unproductive and a waste of time." She sniffs loudly. "We need to figure out a plan of action. We need a lawyer for my husband so we can get him out of jail. We have to figure out why would anybody want to kill my father?"

Carolyn sits next to her. "Helen, did you tell Joshua about the baby?"

"No, they were watching us and listening to everything we said. I almost did, but then I thought that he has enough on his mind. Of course, it might have cheered him up. Did I do, right?"

"I think so, we can tell him when he needs some good news. I wish I could talk to Eddie. He would know what to do. I know he had enough time to get home, after his classes. She stands up. "I am going to ask Matilda if he called." She goes off in the direction of the kitchen. Helen looks at her watch. *It is only half past noon. Today feels like two days long!* She sighs. She might as well as go see her Grand Mamá. She trudges up the wide staircase. Her great grandmother's room is at the top. She knocks lightly. "Gram?" She waits for a response.

"Helen is that you, my dear?" *Her voice seems strong.* Helen thinks.

"May I come in, Grand Mamá?"

"Please, dear, if you would."

Helen slowly turns the knob. She enters the room. "Are you okay, Grand Mamá?" Carolyn Lewis Johnson is sitting with her back to her. She has her long hair down and is brushing it out. She doesn't respond to Helen. She has pins in her mouth to put her hair back up in the Gibson. Helen just stands behind her watching. With practiced motions, it only takes a few moments to complete the look. She pats a stray strand or two then turns to her young great granddaughter and smiles. "My dear girl, where have you been? Have you heard?"

"Yes, Grand Mamá. The police told me at Legacy Plantation and they drove me and Carolyn to be questioned here in EL Dorado. So, I am as good as can be expected. How are you, Grand Mamá?"

"Same. I guess." She stands and goes to Helen and gives her a welcome hug. "I came up here to lay back down. Mattie's wailing was giving me a headache downstairs. I mourn better when I am surrounded by quiet. I take solace in silence."

Helen breaks free. "What will become of everything? Of us?" She asks as she goes to sit on the edge of the made bed, wringing her hands.

"We will go to bed each night and wake up each morning, until we stop hurting so much. I am old and have been through this too many times. It doesn't seem fair that your father is gone at only thirty-four years old and here I am seventy-four and burying yet another loved one. The only thing that I have learned in my long life is that Death is a frequent visitor. This is your second visitation, already." She pauses before going on. "After the shots were fired I ran into your room to see if you were safe. When I saw your bed was undisturbed, I thought you might have been kidnapped by whoever did this. I was sick with worry. Then I realized your bags were gone, too"

"Oh, Gram, I went back to Lawrence to be with my husband. I did not know he was here. Gram, I am going to have a baby. But they have arrested Joshua for Papa's murder. I know he didn't do it. What if I lose my husband, too? How will I raise this one?" She puts her hand protectively over her belly.

"One day at a time, my dear. I thought you might be with child. Kind of caught you off guard, did it?" She puts her arm around her. "You and I must be brave for each other. We have a funeral to plan. You need to call the family lawyer for your husband, if you believe him. You do believe him, then?" Helen nods. "Then I will believe him, also. We will get the best that money can buy. Have you eaten? I think I smell Mattie cooking up something good. Do you get morning sickness?"

"Not so far. I have had a wave of dizziness with a moment or two of nausea but nothing that lasts. I am famished. I haven't eaten since dinner with my Papa." She feels the urge to cry again. *Enough tears!!* "Shall we go down to eat? Carolyn rode with me in the police car and insisted that I see Joshua, before her. I was very jealous of her closeness with my husband, but I misjudged her. I was a fool."

"We are all foolish at different times in life. Learn from it and continue on." She is still holding Helen's hand and gives it a squeeze.

Sullivan has the table set and Matilda is bringing out a large platter of cold sandwiches and behind her is Sullivan carrying a large crock of soup. Helen can hear Carolyn talking to someone.

As Helen is putting her napkin on her lap, Carolyn comes into the dining room, with her husband Eddie. They are arm in arm. Helen feels a pang of jealousy and thinks, *will I have that with Joshua again?* She calls out to Sullivan. "Sullivan get a place setting for my brother Eddie, please."

Eddie rushes to her chair. "I am so very sorry Helen. I just arrived. Anna called me at school and left me a message as soon as you left Lawrence and after I read the note, I cancelled my classes. Anna packed a few things for us, including some reading material to keep our minds off our problems. Carolyn was just filling me in on all that you've been through. I will help however I can. We must get Joshua out of jail and free of these charges. We must get justice for Joshua!"

"Yes, Grand Mamá and I, were just discussing this. After lunch, I will get our lawyers working on Joshua's release. We need to organize Papa's funeral, also." She looks to her sister-in-law, "How will I get through that without my husband?"

As they are just finishing their meal, the doorbell rings. It is Matthew and his wife. As soon as Susan sees Helen, she is crying and hugging. "I told Matthew that I need to be here for you. How can I help?" She finally let's go.

"Where is Katie Ann? I would love to see that ray of sunshine." Helen asks, meekly.

"She is with Judy and Judd. I thought that she would be in the way with all that you have on your mind. Have you heard from Joshua? We can't imagine what's become of him." Helen leads the way to the large parlor. She and Carolyn fill them in on seeing Joshua and hearing that they think the murder weapon is Grant's Navy Colt, taken from the study that was in disarray.

Susan is holding Helen's hand when she says, "what do we

need to do first? Shall I call Funeral Parlor and make arrangements?" She sees Helen look over to the parlor. She can see in Helen's eyes that she is picturing her father's casket there. She says, "Oh, you should NOT have the wake in the parlor. I think too many people will come out of curiosity over the shooting. I can just see them looking around in the woods."

"Grand Mamá, would you mind if Susan helps to set up the wake and funeral? I want to concentrate on Joshua's release."

"I would welcome the help. Thank you, Susan. I think you're right about the wake. My husband and all three children were laid out in the parlor but this was . . . I cannot say the word, but I must . . . this was *murder*." She shivers and tears come to her eyes. "He was a good man, who would want to hurt him? I just cannot understand it."

Eddie speaks up. "I think we need to do our own investigation. With Joshua as the prime suspect, I don't expect them to look any farther for the real killer. On Monday, I will put in for an emergency leave and try to find some answers."

Matthew interrupts him. "I would like to help if I can. I know the prosecutor and he might give me the details on what they have against Joshua. I can't imagine they have anything else."

"They have the murder weapon. Joshua says he was hit over the head at your house Matthew, while getting his suitcase. They found the Colt inside his truck just outside of town."

"He was attacked at my house?" Susan asks shaken. "Why?"

"I imagine to set him up for the murder." Answers Matthew. "We have our work cut out for us. Don't worry Helen. We will figure this out. I would like my Susan to look over the household books for any abnormalities."

"Why? What will that tell you?" Helen asks.

Eddie answers. "The two main reasons for murder are: One) Emotions - that could be love or hate. Two) Money - he either needed it or someone needed it <u>from</u> him. Follow the money trail and you will find the killer."

Helen smiles for the first time, today. "I feel Joshua and I are in good hands, already. You can have access to anything you need. Where do we start?"

Eddie smiles, "We start with a call to your lawyers, ask them to recommend the best criminal defense attorney in Kansas."

Susan asks, "I will call the Funeral Parlor, Aunt Carolyn, do you have a preference as to which one to use? I will start on the books, afterward. I hope I'll recognize 'it' when I see it."

THIRTEEN

An excerpt from Elizabeth Lewis's Journal
Thursday, November 4th, 1880 in Lawrence, Kansas

Life is not fair. It wasn't fair to those Indians nor to my first born and his family.

I suppose I should start telling the Cheyenne tale farther back in time. In the Big Horn Mountains in November of 1876, the Northern Cheyenne's winter camp was destroyed by troops following the last fight of General Custer. The following winter the warrior groups surrender to authorities. They were promised food and fair treatment. In May of 1878, about a thousand Northern Cheyenne left Fort Robinson, Nebraska and walked to the Indian Reservation near Fort Reno. They lost over forty of their number on the way.

They were promised rations by the government but the amount that was delivered was insufficient by half, at least. Testimonies have been given on this to see why what was ordered for the Cheyenne, never reached them. It took only four months for their number to dwindle down to seven hundred or so. They were starving to death, even though they had guns to hunt. They were expert buffalo hunters with no game of any kind to sustain them.

Once the three hundred and fifty-three Cheyenne were afoot, they were chased down by our troops. The squaws dug pits in the ground and hid themselves and their little ones while their braves found higher ground to protect and defend the tribe.

They found some buffalo a few weeks into the journey and they feasted. It was too little too late for many.

Four companies of infantry and some cavalry were dispatched to get them to return to the reservation. Somehow the Cheyenne managed to escape their tracking or when they knew they were close and the braves led them far away from the hiding women, children and elderly.

By the 21st of September they had crossed the Arkansas River and were in Kansas. There was a raid near Sand Creek, Kansas where half of the Cheyenne's few horses were killed before a battle ensued. The tribes managed to flee but the loss of the horses was devastating. Days of walking without the ability of hunting game while on horseback took its toll on the tribe. By the time they reached Decatur County, they were desperate again for food.

The little town of Oberlin, was but twelve miles south of Nebraska, and was just a few months old. That is why the settlers, were eager for the two hundred head of cattle that Ian had brought up. They were given a hero's welcome arriving in town a week ahead of schedule. His drovers were men of experience and the weather cooperated. If they weren't early, the town would have been passed over in the Cheyenne's need for food. All, of those people would be alive today, if only Ian was late instead of early.

Life is not fair, at all.

FOURTEEN

November 5th, 1939,
Sunday in EL Dorado, Kansas

Carolyn woke up in a strange bed at her usual hour, six a.m. Luckily, on the pillow next to her was the man she loved and married.

Eddie heard her wake and turned to her. "We can lay here for another hour, my dear. No one will be up after the late night we had going over the crime scene and the office."

"I know, but I cannot stay asleep any longer." She starts to rise from the bed.

"Carolyn, stay. I know you are worried about Joshua but . . ." He reached for her. She looked at him and she had tears brimming. "My dear. It will be alright. We will do everything in our power to clear him."

She melted back into his arms. "Promise me, Eddie. By all you hold dear, promise me."

With one arm still around her, the other hand swept her bangs out of her eyes. He looked at her gravely. "I promise by everything I hold dear, and I am holding my 'everything dear', this very minute." He kisses her still teary eyes. "Now, no more of these tears." He kisses her sweetly on the lips. "Do I still tickle you?" He is referring to her comment the first time he kissed her. She had said that his black pencil thin moustache tickled her top lip, and she liked it.

"You do more than that, Eddie. Can I tell you a secret?" She asks shyly.

"We have secrets? I thought we knew everything about each other by now." He pretends to be annoyed.

"I was worried that I would be a spinster. I was always told that I was too direct or too 'take charge' to catch a man. In college, I tried to act demure like the silly girls but I couldn't keep up the act. I thought I was doomed. Then you came along and I never had to act dumb or hold myself back."

"This is your secret? Now you are acting like a silly girl. Don't you know that I was dumb-struck by you, the day we met? I was barely able to conduct my class. The more I got to know you, my dear, the more I was hopelessly in love with you. You still amaze me by your strength, brains and your compassion. How you take everyone to your big heart, like Anna and her family. Like Helen, even though she was terrible to you. Your heart is the biggest I have ever had the pleasure to know. You inherited that from the Colonel, I think. And that heart loves me, how lucky can one man be?" He kisses her sweetly. "You do love me, too, don't you, Carolyn?"

"That my beautiful Professor is no secret." She kisses him in return and begins to show her love for him.

Afterward, as they hold each other, and begin to drift back off to sleep, they hear crying from the room down the hall. Carolyn whispers, "I almost forgot that this is a house of mourning. I think that is coming from my Aunt Carolyn. I should go to her."

She quickly dresses and tip toes to her Aunt's room and softly knocks on her door. "Auntie? May I come in?"

She can hear rustling of bedding. "Yes, Carolyn, please come in." As she opens the door, she sees her aunt putting on her robe. Her long hair is down. "Did I wake you with my crying? I am a silly old lady, I am sorry." She goes to her dressing table and starts to comb through her still slightly auburn locks.

"You didn't wake me, I have been up for an hour, already. You're not being silly for mourning the loss of your grandson." She crosses over to her and puts her hand on her shoulder as the older version of herself looks in the mirror.

"I just don't understand why I have had to bury my husband, all three of my children, my daughter-in-law, my granddaughter-in-law, a great grand baby and now my grandson. That is eight caskets that I have had to pick out. You are supposed to bury the generations above you, not below you. I am just so tired of it." She begins to tear again. "NO! My time for crying is done!" She angrily wipes the tear that

65

escapes her eye. "I have another funeral to plan. This will end up the biggest funeral to take place in EL Dorado in quite a while. I thank God that you and your husband are here for Helen. She has been so alone all her life, now she has the big family she deserves." She stands up and kisses her niece on the cheek. "Silly-ness is over. Give me a minute to dress, and put my hair up and we will get Matilda up to make us some coffee. I am nothing without my coffee!"

Carolyn chuckles, "The more I get to know you, Auntie, the more I realize we are cut from the same cloth."

"Well, what other cloth is there? You are a true Lewis, through and through, my dear."

***

By Nine, everyone in the household is up and had breakfast. The family is scheduled to go to the undertakers after the eleven o'clock service at the EL Dorado 1st Congregational Church.

As they arrive to attend service, they are greeted by Anna, Henry and baby Clara Beth. With them are the rest of the Master's clan and Frank Harrick, also. Anna is the first to reach and hug Helen. "My dear, again, I am so sorry. Any word on Joshua, yet?"

All Helen could do is shake her head, no. Carolyn is the next person to get an Anna hug. "Anna, you are a ray of sunshine, this morning." She gladly hugs her back. As she straightens up, she catches the eye of her husband and as he winks at her, she remembers what he said to her this morning, how he said it and she blushes.

Anna looks at her and whispers, "Blushing on a Sunday, Carolyn? And life goes on." She gives her a little elbow in the ribs. "Come, let's get a pew, so we all can sit together."

After service, Judy asks Helen and Carolyn Johnson if they would like to come to the house for a light lunch. Grand Mamá Carolyn answers, "Oh, Judy darling, can we postpone that luncheon? We have an appointment at the Kirby Funeral Home to make arrangements, for my grandson."

Judy nods, "Of course, my dear. We can wait until you are done or if you prefer, you can come for dinner."

Helen is at her great Grand Mamá's side. "That would be wonderful, Judy. By then my husband should be released, to join us."

Judy answers, "I pray it is so, Helen. He doesn't belong there. We all know that. I just wanted to help. If Joshua isn't up to coming over, we can drop the banquet off at your home. I am sure that Matilda needs time to mourn, also. It is the least we can do, at a time like this. Just call us when Joshua comes home and what time you want your supper. Make sure you tell Matilda, not to make anything. I will have enough for her and Sullivan, also."

Helen is overwhelmed by this kindness. "Judy, I do not know what to say."

"Think nothing of it. We are family, that's what family does. Now, call when Joshua is home. Okay?" Judy rubs her arm, then kisses her cheek.

Susan moves forward and takes Helen's arm. "Come cousin, I will go with you and Aunt Carolyn, like I promised."

"Carolyn, can you come with also? I need my sister to stand in for my husband."

"Of course, I am here for you. Anna packed us all more clothing and reading material. Eddie is pulling the car to Henry's truck to get the suitcases, now. Then he will be our chauffer this afternoon.

***

Three hours later, they pull into the long driveway of the Johnson Estate. They are all drained from all the decisions they needed to make. It was so much harder than when the Colonel passed away. The family was prepared for his passing. They knew all his wishes. Helen is not sure if any of the decisions she made would have been what her father wanted.

All Helen wanted was to have Joshua at her side. She asked Matilda if the lawyers called. The answer was no. "Why, they are the most useless . . . !" She slams her fists against the table in frustration and cries out, "I want my husband!!"

"Helen, I have never been so happy to hear those words in my life." They all turn to see Joshua standing in the Parlor.

Helen runs to him. "Joshua, I am so glad you are home. I was so wrong!! I was so foolish. I will never leave you again. I swear it, I love you!!" He is kissing her all over her face and she is crying and kissing him back.

Carolyn turns to Eddie to bury her head into his shoulder. He immediately feels her tears penetrate his shirt. "There, there, Carolyn, Joshua is safe and sound. You are not a crier. What is this?" He removes her head from his wet shoulder so he can look at her.

She wipes her tears away. "I am just so happy he is home!" She says through her continued sobs.

Joshua has left his wife's side and crosses to Carolyn. "Come on sis, it wasn't as bad as that. Now, you are making Helen cry."

"Happy tears, my husband. Very Happy tears!! Did the lawyers bring you home?"

"No, Matthew. He was visiting me when the order for my release came. The attorneys at my arraignment, had me released on my own recognizance. Matthew drove me here so slowly, that I thought I was going to die before I saw you again."

"Honest, he yelled at me to drive faster, at least three times!" Matthew was standing in the doorway. "Then he jumps out of the car, like it was on fire or something. He didn't even let me park! I swear if that doesn't prove he misses you, I don't know what will!" He walks over to Joshua and gives him a small shove. "That's for giving us all a fright, disappearing like that."

"I still have the goose egg to prove someone hit me. I couldn't get the police to feel it so they knew I was telling the truth." He is now rubbing his head.

"Let me take you to the hospital. Let a Doctor check your head for a concussion and get a medical report on file regarding the attack for your defense, at least." Helen says to Joshua.

Matthew says, "I was just going to suggest that. Smart girl!" He gives her a wink.

Joshua says sternly. "Don't you dare flirt with my wife. I am keeping her, if you haven't heard. Besides, your wife is a pretty smart lady herself and they are related, remember?" He now pokes Matthew in the ribs.

Helen looks to her husband. "Joshua, do you want to shower and change before we go to get your head examined?"

"Don't say it like that. I do need to get the jail smell off me. I never thought I would say those words. Matthew, can you get my suitcases? They let me have them when I was released but they kept my truck." He says to Helen. "I'll go up now for that shower. When Matthew brings in my suitcases, will you bring them up to me?" He winks at her.

"Of course, husband, I will be right up!" She says but is blushing in front of her sister-in-law and everyone.

Helen is sitting on the bed, waiting for her husband to come out of the bathroom. *I cannot wait to give him the news!* She is about to burst. *Why was I so upset when I first thought I was with child?* She cannot remember. All that she knows now, is that she and her true love are going to have a baby. She looks down at her still flat belly and says, "I would like to introduce you to someone."

"Who are you talking to?" Joshua is standing at the bedroom door with only a towel on.

"Our little one." She says simply. "You are going to be a father!"

He rushes and kneels at her side. "Helen, are you sure? When did you find out? Are you happy about it?" He pauses a moment. "Is that why you left me? You had second thoughts about me and the baby?" He reaches for her hands and holds them up to his bare chest over his heart.

"I was being stupid. They say women get stupid when they are pregnant. Can I use that as my excuse? I said a lot of things, I didn't mean, Joshua. Can you forgive me?"

"I don't remember any of it. I was hit on the head, you see. Feel it, up here." Now, he moves one of her hands and puts it to his head.

"Oh, Joshua! That IS the size of a goose's egg! We better get you to a doctor, right away."

69

"Helen, I am not going anywhere, right away!" He reaches to caress her face. "Tell me you love me. Tell me that you are mine, forever."

"Forever and ever! I never knew how much, I loved you until you were missing. I was so worried. Do you love me? Forever?"

"I am going to lock the bedroom door and show you just how much I love you. If you don't mind?" He stands up but his towel falls to the ground. Helen giggles as he walks naked to the door to lock it. "Are you laughing at my butt, Mrs. Lewis?"

"No, Mr. Lewis. I wouldn't in a million years." She says as seriously as she can.

FIFTEEN

An Excerpt from Elizabeth Lewis's Journal
Friday, November 5th, 1880 in Lawrence, Kansas

After reading what I have put down so far, I have realized that I still have not told you what has been so devastating to me, though you may have already deduced it. My sorrow and loss came upon the murder of my son Ian, his wife Lydia and their son Joshua Nathaniel.

I did not know how or when exactly they died, even after my Will, then a Major in the Cavalry, went to Oberlin on leave and investigated the scene himself. He believed that they were killed on the 29th because much of the townspeople were found in their Sunday clothing, he was told.

I know that the settlers were killed, their horses taken, and eighty of their cattle were slaughtered to feed to the starving Tribes. I understand their plight, but I think if they had approached them, my son would have offered to help. We have more cattle that we could have resupplied the settlers with, if only they had lived and lost half the herd. It's just not fair. I think their desperation made them assume they must TAKE what was needed.

I must admit my mind understands, but my heart is having a hard time with forgiveness. The Cheyenne were not evil, they were desperate. I have known evil, this was different. I looked in the eyes of pure evil when William Quantrill and his men murdered my neighbors and members of my family. These proud people do not fit into this category.

It was in early October of '78, that Dull Knife and Little Wolf parted from each other. They had decided on different paths for their followers. Little Wolf continued his trek to the ancestral homeland but Dull Knife wanted to go to the Reservation of his kinsmen, the Lakota tribe, at the Red Cloud Agency. He is reported to have said, "Now we have again reached our own ground, and from this time forth we will no more fight or harm any white people." He did not know that the

Lakota were scouting for their 'White Father' and that the Red Cloud Agency was no longer in operation.

On Oct 23, 1878, Dull Knife's tribe walked into an area surrounded by Companies B & D of Carlton's 3rd Cavalry. They were patrolling the White River area near Fort Robinson in Nebraska. The Cheyenne were expected to pass through the area and the homesteader's and settlers were being given extra protection in case of Indian attack.

After days of negotiation with Dull Knife and his 148 followers, they were sent to Fort Robinson to be held under the authority of Maj. Caleb H. Carlton. They were told that they were to be quartered there for at least three months. Relief was felt through the small tribe. Warmth and food would be supplied during the heart of winter. They were allowed hunting rifles, (though many pistols and rifles were hidden among the clothing and blankets). They were told that they would be treated as prisoners of war but they could hunt for themselves. As long, as every brave and squaw was accounted for at the dinner roll-call, they would have this freedom.

In December, after they were comfortably settled in the different lodges at the prison, Major Carlton was sent to hunt Little Wolf and a Captain Henry W. Wessells, Jr. was sent as temporary commander of Fort Robinson. He was told that the Cheyenne must return to the Southern Reservation but Wild Hog and about five of other braves would be taken to Fort Wallace to await trial for the murder of my son and all the other settlers.

By this time the snows were heavy on the land and Dull Knife and Wild Hog (a brave of increasing influence among the tribe) refused to allow their people to make that trip. The weather would surely kill them and if they did make the trek, the barren land would finish off the rest.

Wild Hog reportedly declared, "this is our home. Here we have been raised. Here we have buried our fathers and our children! We cannot live in the Indian Territory. If you will allow us to remain we will do anything the Great Father may require of us. We will live like white people, work and wear their clothes. We will never make trouble."

If only they had been allowed to do this. Again, the minds

of the Indian Affairs people baffle me.   This was not an unreasonable request as long, as those who killed the settlers were made to stand trial.   But, alas it was not to be and it almost cost me a second son.

SIXTEEN

November 6th, 1939
Monday in EL Dorado, Kansas

Last night, Helen had taken Joshua to the Susan B. Allen Memorial Hospital to have his lump examined and to see if he had a concussion. They didn't go to her great uncle Doc Johnson's clinic, so that the medical evidence wouldn't look suspect or 'doctored'. The fact that Joshua lost consciousness for a few hours worried the Doctor but now that almost twenty-four hours have passed since the attack, he doesn't feel the need to keep him, overnight. Aspirin for the headache was prescribed but nothing else.

When they arrived back at the Johnson farmhouse, the driveway was filled with vehicles. The Masters made good on their offer to bring food, it seemed. The clan did not stay long. They just wanted the Johnson/Lewis family including Matilda and Sullivan well fed and feeling loved and not alone during their time of bereavement.

Helen had a restless night sleep. She dreamt that her father was calling to her and she woke and cried in Joshua's arms. Joshua whispered. "I wish he had let me stay that night. I might have prevented his murder. I am so sorry, my love. Why do you think he refused me like that? He didn't know that you went to Lawrence, so why did he try to keep me from you?"

"My poor Papa, I wonder if he knew or had a feeling and wanted you out of harm's way?"

"But, if he was expecting you to come home, then you were in harm's way! That can't be it. Any other thoughts?"

"Just that I wish I had said good-bye." She starts to sob again.

The morning in the Johnson Farmhouse was a busy one. Somehow, the news spread about Grant's murder and the RKO News Agency was parked at the entrance of the Johnson Estate after being chased away with a 'no comment' from the household occupants.

Carolyn and Eddie were up at their usual early hour and Eddie dressed immediately and went into Grant's study to call the University to ask for an emergency leave of absence. He was transferred to the Dean of the University, himself, before he was given permission.

The Funeral Director, Paul Kirby, arrived at 9:30, as promised, to pick out a suit from Grant's closet. This personal attention is always afforded to the elite. Sullivan shows him to the room and while Helen watches with tears in her eyes, as he pulls out several suits and lays them across the bed. Mr. Kirby selects a brown tweed one. Helen crosses the room, to feel the heavy fabric. "Papa should stay warm in this for winter." She looks to Sullivan. "I don't recall seeing Papa in this suit, is it new?"

"Yes, Missus. He just ordered it a few weeks ago. Told me it was his new favorite. Pity that he won't get to see himself in it." Sullivan suddenly sniffs loudly and turns away from Helen. Without looking at her, he says, "Can you excuse me Ma-am, for a moment. I will be back to show Mr. Kirby to the door." He sniffed once more as he left without waiting for Helen to answer.

Mr. Kirby looks up at Helen. "It says much of a man when the servants are mourning as hard as the family." He has brought a small suitcase and carefully folds the suit into it. He picks out a shirt and tie and puts them in the case also. "Was Mr. Johnson a man who was comfortable with jewelry? Did he wear a ring, perhaps? It would be just for the wake. We would return it to you prior to taking him to his final resting place. I understand that he was a widower but did he have a wedding ring?"

Helen had to think about this a moment. Her father used to have a small gold band. "He did wear one but I do not think that it fits him, anymore. He has gained weight since my mother passed."

"If you'd like him to wear it, we could . . . um . . . make it fit." Though it is his job to discuss personal details with the grieving, he seems very uncomfortable with this subject. He keeps adjusting his tie as if it is suddenly trying to strangle him.

"He did talk about getting it sized so that he could wear it again. I think he would like to see my mother again with his ring on. We will leave it on, I think." She goes to the dresser and pulls out a jewelry box from the top drawer. She sees the ring and hands it to him. "He needs his favorite tie clip and cuff links, also." She hands those to him, too.

"Very well, Madame. As you wish."

Helen goes back to the suits left on the bed. She picks one up and holds it against herself. "It still smells like my Papa. What will I do with all these things?" She asks aloud, not expecting an answer.

Susan comes to go over the books at 10 a.m. Matthew was with her. They all crowd into Grant's study to look in the files for anything suspicious. Susan decides to take the ledger into the dining room to get privacy so that she can concentrate and spread out. She doesn't know what she is looking for but Matthew assured her, she will know it when she sees it. Before she repositioned herself, she asked Matthew to find all bank statements so that she can make sure she knows what account paid what expenses.

When Matthew brings her the bank statements, she asks "What about the business books? Do you handle those at the farm office or does Grant keep them here?"

"Actually, Pa does the farm business books."

Helen has gotten a hot cup of tea from the kitchen and is sitting at the far end of the dining room table to drink it. The appointment with the Funeral Director exhausted her. She looks at Susan reading the ledger then comparing the debits with the statements. She doesn't interrupt their conversation and they are too engrossed in it to notice her sitting there.

"I was just wondering if we should look at those, also." Susan continues, "If nothing jumps out of the household accounts, that is"

"Grant has given over everything farm related to us to do. He was a very busy man and relied and completely trusted my father with the total management of the farm. He hardly came to the farm office at all the last couple of years."

Helen almost spits out her tea. Matthew and Susan are startled. Matthew says, "Are you okay, Helen?"

"Did you say that my father hardly went to the farm office? How long did you say that was happening?"

"I can tell you exactly. It was right after we found out Anna was alive. After we came home from her wedding in Lawrence, Grant sat us down and told us that he was going to invest his time in other projects. He said that, since getting to know us during the year that Anna was missing, he came to trust our judgement completely. He wanted my father to run everything. He expected Pa to make detailed reports, but he only came in to read them about once a month. That started the last week of September in 1936."

"What 'other projects' was he doing?"

"You don't know?" Susan asks Helen.

"I have no idea. He got up and dressed and left every morning for the farm office, then came home in time for dinner at 6. Where was he every day?"

Matthew looks at her, "why do I have the feeling that if we figure that out, we will find a reason for his murder!" He stands and goes into the study to talk with Eddie.

Eddie and Matthew come out of the study together. "Where is Sullivan?" Helen gets up and goes to the pull cord. Just moments later, Sullivan silently appears. Eddie pulls out two dining room table chairs and turns them around to face each other and sits down on one, lazily. "Sullivan, we were just discussing Mr. Johnson's activities. Could you enlighten us on his daily schedule? Have a seat." He motions to the seat in front of him. Sullivan sits. "Susan, do you have a pen?" She hands it to him. Eddie takes a notebook out of his pocket. "Okay, Sullivan. What did Mr. Johnson do all day?"

"Well, sir. I helped him dress every morning at 6:30. Then he had breakfast. He might go in his study for a moment or two, but he was usually out the door by 7:30. He would always be back home so we could serve dinner at 6 p.m. sharp."

Eddie leans forward and puts his elbows on his knees. "Sullivan, we know that part, but I asked you was _what_ did he do all day?"

Sullivan looks around at all the faces in the room watching him. "Sir, I don't understand what you askin' me, sir?"

"I am asking you, where he went when he left, and what did he do?"

"He went to the farm office to work, sir."

Helen goes to him and kneels at his feet. "Sullivan, we are just curious. He only went to the farm office once a month. Where was he the rest of the time? If you know, please tell us. He is gone; you do not have to keep his secrets anymore."

"Mistress Helen, don't *you* know what he did?" She shakes her head no. "You wuz the closest person to him, 'cept hiz Grand Mamá. If you did not know, why woulds I?" He was becoming emotional. "He wuz my very own little baby brother, growing up, but he wuz my better. Iz saw him go through the death of hiz aunts, hiz mother and father, and then the loss of your mother and little baby, but he did not talk to me, *that way*, Mistress. He wuz such a smart man, and always kind. But, he never did tell me about hiz work or that he weren't going to the office. Iz just thought he wuz, Mistress Helen." A tear escapes his eye. Helen stood up but bent over to hug him. "It's okay, Sullivan. We will figure this out.

Eddie stands up and puts his hand on Sullivan's shoulder. "You're a good man, Sullivan. I am sure that Grant appreciated all you did. You may go, but if you think of anything to help us – please do not hesitate to tell us."

Sullivan gets up and uses his large hands to wipe his tears, then turns to the room's occupants. "He did become awful quiet in the evenings after you wuz married, Mistress. He would sit in hiz study in the dark, many a night. Maw and I worries'd about him. Mrs. Carolyn had her social life, but Master Grant, stayed in the dark." He turned back and left the room.

Helen sat down. "My poor father, he must have been depressed after I left."

"NONSENSE!!" Grand Mamá Carolyn said, standing in the doorway with her hands on her hips. "I know depression, and my Grandson was not depressed. My mother suffered from depression for years after my brother's murder. Grant never had any of her symptoms. Sullivan is overly dramatic! Always has been. Grant had a few headaches in the evenings. He said that handling all the details of the farm sometimes got to him."

Helen explains, "But, Grand Mamá, father didn't take care of the farm any more. I just found out that he let Judd and Matthew run it day to day *for three whole years*! He has only checked in there, once a month or so. Where did he go each day, we were wondering?"

The elder Carolyn crosses the room and looks out the window. The sun seems to be bothering her eyes. She blinks repeatedly. "When I asked about his health, he always used the farm as an excuse. I wonder if . . . it cannot be that!" She suddenly holds onto the curtain, then tries to steady herself with both hands on the table in front of the window. Helen and Eddie rush to her because she looks as if she is about to swoon.

"Grand Mamá, what is it?" Helen asks, "Are you faint?" They help her across the hall to the parlor and place her on the couch. Helen fans her with a magazine from the coffee table. "Are you better? Do you want a glass of water, maybe?"

"Helen, I just had the most heart-wrenching thought. Your father was getting THE headaches. He was disappearing every day to hide them, I think."

Helen loses all color in her fair face, too. She just barely manages to lower herself down next to her great-grandmother. Joshua and his sister come into the parlor. Joshua sees his wife and goes to her. "Helen, are you sick? What is going on?"

She looks up at him with such sadness, her eyes brimming with tears. "My father knew he was dying." She barely got the words out before she and her great-grandmother turn to each other and cry on each other's shoulders. Everyone else in the room just stand there, confused.

Joshua is still kneeling beside the sofa. "I don't understand Helen. Please try to explain." He hands her his handkerchief.

She wipes her eyes and her nose, then blows before speaking. "His headaches weren't just headaches. They were the family curse. BRAIN CANCER. Both of my Great Aunts died long and agonizing deaths from it."

Grand Mamá interrupts, "It was awful watching my girls die that way. In 1922, my Ada having had suffered from migraines for years, became delirious from the constant pain. She moaned and wailed at all hours; it was torture to watch and not be able to help. The last three months were so bad that her brother and I put her in a sanitarium where they kept her in a constant drugged state, but it still did not take all the pain away. After she passed, at only 38 years old, they performed an autopsy and saw the cancer and all the damage that it caused. A year later, my daughter Ida started with the headaches. She suffered the same fate as her sister, and died at 40 years old in the same sanitarium in 1925." Grand Mamá put her head in her hands, and her body heaved as she broke down in sobs, again.

"My father must have known and hid it from us." She looks at her Grand Mamá. "He loved us so much to spare us this awful news, but it explains the missing hours, the lying and the headaches. *Oh, Papa!*"

They all take a moment to digest this sad revelation. The silence is broken by Susan. "That still doesn't explain his murder."

SEVENTEEN

An Excerpt from Elizabeth Lewis's Journal
Saturday, November 6, 1880 in Lawrence, Kansas

Captain Wessler, it turns out was a very mean man. He was under orders to force the Cheyenne back to the Reservation on the Indian Territory. He was the Commander of Fort Robinson for only a short time, when he decided that the Cheyenne needed less firewood to aid in their decision-making process. While their young and old ones shivered; they refused to go.

Weeks passed. He then thought that less rations would help them decide to go back. The Braves and Squaws would give their food to the young ones, while they themselves went hungry. And yet, they still refused to go.

Two more weeks past. Finally, Captain Wessler, locked them all in one lodge and told them no one would eat or have firewood until they agreed to go back. Outside, the snow drifts continued to rise as the temperature continued to fall.

The final straw that left them no alternative but to plan their escape from Fort Robinson was the with-holding of water from the tribe. Locked in with no firewood, no food, and now - no water! Who wouldn't make a desperate attempt at freedom?

On January 9th, they boldly overpowered the guards and fled to the hills and bluffs but many were shot down within a mile or so from the fort.

My son, Major William Lewis was sent to Fort Robinson to pursue the Cheyenne in January of 1879 under the order of General George Crook. He was sent with two fresh companies of 3rd Cavalry.

It was devastating news to learn that my Will would be off hunting and possibly fighting the very ones that killed my first-born. The only thing that helped me cope was the surprise that Will had arranged.

An excerpt from the Letters of
Major William Lewis

Jan 12, 1879

Dear Julia,

Cousin, May I still call you that? We used that as a term of endearment that I do not want to presume I still have a right to hold. I know that it's been several years since we have last communicated and it is my sincerest regret that it is all my fault, MY most grievous fault.

Mother has told me of your letter to her of sympathy on our family's tragedy. It warms my heart that you were so kind to do so. Mother has always held you in the highest regards.

The reason for this letter is two-fold. I wanted to thank you for your kindness shown to Mother and to ask for yet another kindness to her.

I have just received word that I am to travel to Nebraska to take over the command of the 3rd Cavalry. It seems that the Cheyenne that were responsible for my brother's death have escaped Fort Robinson and I am to lead the charge to hunt them down. I must leave by tomorrow evening.

The favor that I ask is that you find it in your heart to go and stay with my mother during this hard time for her. My siblings have tried to fill the void left by the absence of Ian's family but are not able to get past the loss themselves. I fear that my departure will add worry to her sorrow and I would not want that for a minute. I feel your presence will be of great comfort to her as she always felt that you were another of her daughters and having you back, will bring her more than a little joy in her life.

I know that I am asking the largest of favors, considering that I have failed to keep in contact with you and your brother Grant over the last several years since he inherited the family estate. I promised both of you that I would stay in touch and the only explanation I have for my failure is that my youth did not know a good thing until it moved away. Then, when my youth felt the pain of your absence, it decided to ignore the hurt and in doing so I ignored the BEST thing that ever happened to my childhood and my life.

I know that you have not held my objectionable actions from continuing to stay in contact with my Mother and my sisters Lizzie, Marjorie or Carolyn. I hope and pray that you will consider this as a favor to them and not to me, as I am not worthy of any favors from you or your family.

I do not know how long this campaign will keep me away from Lawrence. I know that I must leave as soon as possible, that is why I have sent this note by messenger. I asked the courier to wait for a return message. Please tell me that you will come visit my mother. I would like to give her this good news when I give her the bad news of my departure.

Grandmother Marilyn says that she would love to have you visit with her and Grandfather Clyde. They are getting on in years and miss you terribly also.

I do not know how else to convince you to do this for my mother, other than offering one comforting note. You will not have to look upon my inexcusable person during your stay, as I expect that this campaign will keep me away from home all the way till spring, at least.

Thank you for taking the time to read this lengthy correspondence. Please give your written answer to the courier. Please let it be a yes!!

Yours very truly,

Major Wm. Lewis

An excerpt from the letters of Julia Johnson

January 12, 1879

Dearest Will,

Dearest, Dearest Cousin, you may still call me that term of endearment as we still share the same grandparents and share the same feeling of loss caused by the separation from one other. Since the man you hired is waiting for my answer, I must rush all the words that I want to say to you. There is too much to say in so short a time.

I am thrilled that you regret your neglect of myself and my brother Grant. In Lawrence, growing up, you followed him like a puppy dog and when you did not return his letters he took great offense. Then, when one of your sisters would write of your great escapades, he would forgive you, for all your adventures.

As far as those adventures are concerned, and I have no right to ask you this, but I was under the assumption that you had found love while in Fort Leavenworth. Is this true? If so, I am glad for you but sad for the us that almost was and COULD HAVE BEEN.

Putting all that aside, my answer is such - I will prepare to leave for Lawrence as soon as is possible. I will pack in preparation to stay until spring. I so hope to see you before I come back to El Dorado. Or if your campaign keeps you longer, may-haps you can visit us here. I long to see you, if only to give my dear sweet cousin a hug for being such a good and caring son. Your mother always told me that you had a heart as big as they come and by this request, I think that it proves it, rightly so.

Yours very truly,
Julia

EIGHTEEN

November 7th, 1939
Tuesday in EL Dorado, Kansas

Even with the reading about the reconnecting of the Colonel and his Julia last night, Helen had trouble sleeping, again. After learning of her father's illness, she tried to replay all the moments and discussions that she had had with her father. In hindsight, there were plenty of clues. *Hindsight is a terrible choice of words.* It was her father's eye trouble that should have told her everything. He had a look of dull pain behind his eyes and would blame it on the electric lights, or the sun or dust but never a headache. *How terribly brave he was,* she thinks.

Sleeping is also elusive, due to her dread of the upcoming events. Today and tomorrow will be her father's wake, to be followed by the funeral service on Thursday. She didn't know how she will be able to hold up during the greeting of the long lines of mourners that will surely show up. *How will I get through it?* She wonders.

Also, yesterday, Joshua got a call from the lawyers. His Preliminary Hearing for trial will be on Friday. This made everyone want to work overtime to find the real killer.

Matthew, Eddie and Susan spent all of yesterday afternoon and much of this morning trying to go through every scrap of paper in the study, desperately looking for a money trail, as the Professor explains it. They still had much to do.

Helen wanted to help and become somewhat abreast of the financial situation that she will inherit. She just could not concentrate on it. The thought of her father's ailment just tormented her. *He suffered in silence, he did it all for me,* she kept thinking.

Mr. Kirby suggests the family come to the funeral home at 2:30 in the afternoon for a private family viewing. When they pull up to the Kirby Funeral Home on South Star St., Helen stares at the Colonial Front of the two-story building. "Grand Mamá, was this the Byrd Funeral Home that my Mama and brother were at? I don't know why I didn't notice this before."

"My Girl, you remember the building? You were barely ten years old." She squeezes her hand. "It is amazing what the mind grabs on to and locks away. It has been the Kirby Home for several years now. But, why would you know that? A girl your age, doesn't attend these things as often as someone my age. F. M. Byrd was the Funeral Director for my husband in 1910 as well as with each of my children."

Helen and her Grand Mamá entered the parlor holding each other's hands for support. Helen felt as if she was holding her breath. She hoped that she will be able to control her emotions for the sake of her Grand Mamá. Joshua had his hand on her shoulder from behind her. There were flowers everywhere, especially in the alcove where the casket lay. Between them and the casket were rows and rows of chairs, all lined up waiting for mourners. She heard herself say, "Ready, Gram?" She got the reply by getting her another squeeze of her hand.

They take small steps. Joshua now has his arm around her waist. He bends over to whisper. "Breathe Helen, we don't want you to pass out." She takes in a large breath but instead of exhaling she holds that one in, also. Tears are starting to form in her eyes. She hesitates. Both her husband and her great-grandmother stop to look at her. Joshua turns to her again. "It will be okay, Helen. Exhale, please." She looks up at him and laughs. His cheeks were all puffed out and he makes a very dramatic expulsion of the air. "There, that's better. See I am here for you, darling."

As they are approaching, Helen concentrates on her steps, her breathing, then the flowers surrounding the casket. It isn't until she can reach out and touch it's elegant wood does she look at her father. She wanted to shake him and tell him to wake up. "Papa, please," is all she could say. She hears the sobs from her Gram. She squeezes her hand and turns to her. "It will be okay." Knowing that it will be a very long time before this will be true.

There is another sob to her left. She turns to see tears streaming down her husband's face. *No, I can take anything but to see him cry!* "Oh, Joshua, he loved you too." All her husband could do is nod. He backed up a foot to give her room.

She let go of her Gram's hand and supported herself on the casket, looking closely now at her father. The left side of his head looked funny, they applied too much make-up to hide a bruise on his cheek and his hair was combed too far back. "Papa, you didn't wear your hair like this." She opens her purse and takes out a comb and runs it through his hair, and brings some of his bang to cover his forehead. "There Papa, that looks better." She pats him on the shoulder. "I like your new suit. The light color brown makes your hair look more golden." She is talking to him as if he will answer. "Who did this to you, Papa? Why? Please give us some clues. Otherwise, they will lock up my husband and your grandchild will lose both men that would have love him the most. And I will lose both men that I love the most! Please, Papa. Help us solve your murder." She reaches out and holds his hands. *Mr. Kirby did get the wedding ring on him.* She rubs it, lovingly. "Papa, I love him as much as you loved Mommy. Don't let him get taken from me. I won't survive without either of you." She can't control herself now. *"Papa, please, help me!!"*

Joshua moves to go to her but her Gram is there first. "He will send us the answers, my dear. I know he will. He loved us too much, not to do everything to help us." This calms her down. She turns away from her father and wipes her face.

Mr. Kirby is standing nearby with a box of tissues, at the ready. "There, there, my dear, your father wouldn't want to see you fret so."

She takes a tissue and nods to him. She blows her nose. "How much time do we have before we have to let the mourners in?"

He looks at his pocket watch. "A half an hour, my dear. There is still time."

She looks at him. "You don't understand, it will take my nose an hour for the color to return to normal." She smiles as she sees him smile. "Thank you sir. I didn't quite realize why we had a private time with our loved one, before the outsiders, come in. I needed this. Will I have private time to say good-by, before the casket is closed?"

"Yes, my dear, you will have private time each night, then on Thursday, we will have a small prayer gathering, then they will file out and you will have time for a private good-bye, then we close the casket and transport it to the church for the Funeral service. After that, we go straight to the Cemetery for that service. Any other questions?"

"Do I have to greet all the mourners? I don't know if I will be able to hold up." Then she adds as an explanation. "I am newly with child."

"Poor child, this will be hard. Remember that the mourners are here to show their respect to your father, and your family. Someone, should be available to thank them for coming but it doesn't have to be you, all the time. The closest family members usually sit in the front row between turns at the reception line. You can only do what you can do and no more. It has been my experience that mourners understand."

"Thank you, Mr. Kirby. You have been most kind." She holds out her hand to shake his.

He takes it and shakes it. "No thanks, needed. I am honored, to serve is my job. Now if you'd like to powder your nose. The ladies room is this way." He leads her to the lavatory.

***

Hours drag on. Helen shakes many hands but Joshua and his sister, Carolyn, insist that she sit and rest, out of sight of the mourners, for several minutes each hour. Helen saw many people that she knows, childhood friends, associates of her fathers, acquaintances of her Gram's, etc.

The Butler County's longest serving District Attorney came to pay his respects to the Grant Johnson family. He had been the attorney that prosecuted the two men that robbed the Johnson Family Farm paymaster's office in 1935. Matthew was the star witness in both those prosecutions. He was also the Prosecutor of John Walker, Anna's attacker in 1937. Matthew and Susan, Anna's sister Melinda, as well as Anna and Henry all testified in that trial. He approached Matthew who automatically gave his 'handshake to a hug' welcome that he gives to those he admires and respects. After Anthony Pollock speaks briefly to the Masters family members, he pays his respects to the Johnson family. A short time later, Matthew pulls him to the side to ask him what he knows about the upcoming prosecution of Joshua Lewis.

Helen survives the long hours of the first day. After the last mourners leave, she and her Gram are given a moment to say good-night to the beloved man in the casket. Helen leans over and kisses his cheek. "Papa, you are so cold. I will see you tomorrow, okay?" She pats his hands, rubbing his ring, again. "Thank you for helping me today. I felt your strength, all day." She kisses him, again. "Continue to help me, please Papa?" She gives him a final pat on his shoulder before she turns to cry on her husband's shoulder, as he leads her out.

NINETEEN

An excerpt from Elizabeth Lewis's Journal.
Sunday, November 7th, 1880 in Lawrence, Kansas

It was very shortly after my son Will left in January 1879 when Julia Johnson arrived. She had grown only slightly taller than myself but she looked so grown up that I hardly recognized her. My younger girls were all so happy to have their favorite cousin back in Lawrence. Lizzie and Joseph were both in Wichita at the Medical Practice in which they were partners, so the house had a sense of fullness again with Julia's presence.

Will left to command the 3rd Cavalry to search for the remaining Cheyenne that had escaped capture in the wilderness of Nebraska. By all accounts the winter storms were as much an enemy to the troops as they were to the Cheyenne.

I secretly prayed that none of the braves would survive to be captured, and then I would beg forgiveness from our Lord for being so vengeful. If the braves did not survive, what would happen to the innocent children or the women? They had all been through so much, how could I ask God to put more on them?

I was almost happy with Julia staying with us, but I worried so for Will, that once again, I slept very little. We all got so excited if a letter came from him or Joseph or Lizzie. We each would read them out loud as if they were a great piece of literature, instead of siblings scribbling to each other, except for the letters Will wrote to his Julia

An excerpt from the letters of
Major William Lewis

January 29th, 1879

Dearest Julia,

Cousin, I am so relieved that you have arrived safely to the arms of my Mother. She sent a telegram to Fort Robinson, notifying me of your arrival. I am sure that my sisters are, by now, becoming a source of exasperation, with their silliness. It is funny, I do not recall you ever being in that silly stage that they have perpetually been in.

My recollections, are becoming my warmth in this dreaded cold Nebraska winter. I and my men are out on patrols and in scouting parties at all hours. We are miles away from any known hospitality. During the long hours of cold winds blowing in my face while I search the countryside for these renegades, a fleeting memory of you creeps into my thoughts, and with it comes a slow warmth that does my spirit as well as my body much good.

The other day, two of my youngest privates started a feud over something and it escalated into a snowball fight. Soon half the company was lobbing frozen compact balls at each other, all in good fun. As I sat back on my horse and watched the nonsense, a memory of you surfaced and I swear a smile reached my lips and almost cracked my frozen cheeks off. May I tell you of it?

Do you remember in the 9th grade when your friend Sally said something that got you so mad that you tried to hit her with a snowball? You tried to throw it so hard that you lost your footing on the snow-covered ground that hid the ice beneath and you fell backwards into a snowdrift. The freshly fallen snow engulfed you and I could barely find you but when I rescued you from your snowy burial, you put your arms around me and gave me my first kiss. My cheeks are burning now just thinking about it.

As I have written this, I half forgot that by reminding you

91

of these treasured moments, I would also be reminding you that I abandoned you when you moved to El Dorado. I do hope that you have looked in your heart and sought to forgive me.

You see, I am truly pleading for that forgiveness. I do not think that I can look upon your beautiful countenance knowing that you might be harboring disappointment, or worse, hate for me because of my carelessness.

When I sent the courier with my letter to you, your letter came back with a question in it that I have not yet addressed. You asked if I found love at Fort Leavenworth. I must be honest. I had formed a very strong bond with a young lady there. She talked of a future for us, but that was before my brother and his family were killed. I wrote her a note ending any thoughts she might have of a future when the courier came back with your answer. My relationship with her was but a trifle, as I started to recall all the moments that YOU made special.

All those moments that made up my childhood from the first time I saw you at seven years old at my Grandfather Clyde's wedding to your Grandmother Marilyn. All those moments! There is nothing and no one that can compare!

I know that I have no right to assume that those moments meant as much to you as they did to me but if there is the slightest possibility that they did or do . . . and if you can find it in your heart to forgive me . . . Here I am being so bold without the slightest bit of encouragement.

I pray that I am not offending you. If so, I pray that you will forgive me. I pray that you still think of me as the one who could make all those moments special again. I pray that this finds you in the best of health and that you will still be in Lawrence when this campaign comes to an end. Or if not, I pray that you will welcome me for a visit in El Dorado as soon as I am free to do so. I pray that I may look upon your loveliness, once again, if not for anything other than that hug you spoke of in the courier's note.

Yours very truly,
Major Wm. Lewis

TWENTY

November 8th, 1939
Wednesday in EL Dorado, Kansas

Matthew and Susan are at the Johnson Estate farmhouse at 9 a.m. sharp. Susan is holding little Katie Ann. Sullivan lets them in, but Matilda is at the door faster than anyone knew she could move!

"Lil' Katie Ann!! Come to Matilda." She holds out her arms and Katie Ann goes willingly to her. "Just a breath of sunshine, just like her mama wuz! Sullivan, remember her curls wuz just as blonde and unruly. I never understood how curly hair can be so light! But our Master Grant wuz the same, don't you 'member?" She looks up at Susan. "Can I take her in the kitchen and gives her some cookies, they iz fresh from the oven?" Then she looks at the little one. "You'd like some cookies, Katie Ann?" Katie Smiles. "Sullivan, look at that smile. It can lighten the heaviest heart!! Thank you, Missus Susan for bringing her." She is bouncing the child in her arms.

Susan smiles at the sight. "Like I had a choice, Matilda. You pleaded with me daily. It grew tiresome!" As Matilda turns toward the kitchen bouncing the babe on her hip, Susan calls after her. "Just one of those cookies, Mattie. She ate a good breakfast, already and I know how large your treats are!" Matilda continues walking away, without hesitating. Once gone, Susan says, "I hope she heard me."

Helen comes in the room, smiling. "She might have but she wouldn't listen, if she did. She thinks roly-poly babies are healthy." She hugs her cousin. "Thank you for bringing her. I hope that I get a chance to hold her for a minute, if we can get Matilda to let her go."

Joshua is behind her. "Eddie and Carolyn will be down in a minute. Eddie said you talked to Mr. Pollock, last night about the case?" He says as a question.

"Yes, and unfortunately, it is not good. Sullivan – lots of strong coffee, please. We are going to need it."

93

As they are all at the dining room table and have had a second pot of coffee with lots of cups poured, Helen thought that Matthew was delaying the inevitable. "Matthew, please just tell us. What is the case against my husband?"

"I don't know how to tell you, Helen. It seems that you are a very wealthy woman." He smiles, weakly.

"I've known that for a while, Matthew." She says with a small blush.

"But did you know that your father had a large insurance policy?" She shakes her head, no.

"With the notoriety of the case, the insurance company has gone to the police. It seems that Grant took out a policy above and beyond the normal amount. This is the money trail that the police are wrongly following. They are building the case that Joshua killed your father for your Insurance inheritance."

She smiles hesitantly, "it would have to be a large one for my Joshua to be tempted." She looks at Matthew who isn't smiling back. "How much is it?"

"One million dollars."

Joshua was just lifting his coffee cup up and drops it down to the saucer. All look to him, he is white as a ghost. "I am doomed! How can I fight that figure?"

Helen begins to sob. "I'll give the money to charity – It is blood money if it takes my husband from me and the baby!"

Joshua leaves his seat to go to her. He kneels next to her chair. "I am here now, Helen. They will find a way to save me." He sounds very sure of that fact then looks at the faces of the team. Eddie, his sister Carolyn, Matthew, Susan and even Grand Mamá Carolyn look beaten. "Right guys?" His voice is now shaking.

Matthew speaks up. "I won't give up. Their money trail is a dead end. It isn't the cause of the murder so we must keep digging."

Eddie says, "I still think that his daily false routine is somehow connected. He had to go somewhere and someone else had to know about it. Two years is a long time to drive around for eight hours. There would be wear and tear on the vehicle and gasoline charges that would be noticeably higher.

If he had a room somewhere, someone would think it suspicious that the wealthiest farmer in the county needed a flat. We need to look for someplace he owned. What about all the farm properties?" Eddie looked to Matthew. "Are there any year-round homes on the ones you know about?"

"Grant always tore down any farmhouse on the property. Having bought so many farms from the bank, the houses on the land were usually dilapidated. I would have to double check with Pa. Even if there was a home on one of the active farms, the chances of getting discovered would be huge."

Helen stands up and everyone looks to her. "Papa has a file for the property tax bill receipts. Maybe we can sort them out and see which ones would have a house."

She heads over to her father's study. Susan gets up from the table and follows her. They are gone for a few minutes and when they come back both have their hands full of papers.

Susan says, "Grant sure owned enough properties. These are all the paid tax bills! The papers seemed in no kind of order at all. Within a few minutes, they had neat piles on the dining room table. Each pile was a specific property. "The problem is that only a few of these have actual addresses on them; most only have a legal description. Matthew, I think you and Pa are going to have to figure out which ones are working farm land with houses." She looks, again, at one small pile. "This stack of receipts is different."

Matthew leans over, "What's different about them?" He is looking from one pile to the next.

"Don't you see it?" Helen and Joshua are now up trying to determine the difference.

Helen exclaims, "Oh, that doesn't make sense, why would he only pay these in cash, in person and the rest have check numbers on them?"

Matthew looks at Susan and Helen, then at Joshua. "I knew my Susan would find it. Helen, you are obviously, related to her. Good job, Ladies."

"But what did we find?" Susan asks.

"Grant's daytime hide away." Matthew sits back in his chair. "I have a job to do, after the funeral, tomorrow."

Eddie is looking at the receipts. "These don't have an address on them."

"I know, I have to go to the accessor's office to find out the address AND since I don't think Grant went to pay these, himself, maybe, they will tell me who his accomplice is."

Joshua smiles. "See Helen, I am in good hands." She weakly smiles back.

"I know Joshua, but Matthew reminded me of something. Tomorrow is my father's funeral. Your Preliminary Hearing is the day after that. There isn't much time."

Matthew looks at his watch. It is not yet noon. "Why don't I take Katie Ann home and drop her off with Ma, then pick up Pa and drive to the Assessor's office today. I will take all the bills without addresses with me, in case, we are wrong. Pa and I can go over them to try and figure out if any have houses or other structures are on the properties that Grant could stay in. We will meet you at the wake, afterward. Then we will have a jump on it all."

***

Matthew and his Pa, Judd, are at the Butler County Assessor's Office by two p.m. They have figured out several of the property locations from their farm records, even though they only have the legal description. They still have four properties that they do not know 'which is which' and that includes the cash-paid-in-person property.

They must wait in line and it is nearly thirty minutes before it is their turn. As they lay out the papers on the counter, Matthew smiles and says. "I sure hope you can help us. We are the managers of the Johnson Family Farms and with the death of the owner, Grant Johnson, we are trying to get everything organized for whoever is going to inherit. As you know, the Johnson holdings are numerous but these four properties are unknown to us. Well, we know them, but we don't know which one is which, if you know what I mean. Could you tell us the street address of each and if possible how long the property has been owned by Grant Johnson?" He gives her a little wink. Loretta is wearing a name tag and is smiling back at the tall, dark, and handsome twenty-year old, with the clear blue eyes. "This would mean so much to us, Loretta. We want to be able to look knowledgeable to the new owners, you know?"

She takes the papers from him and goes to a very large ledger on the back desk. She is there for a few moments looking up each of the four properties. She writes on a piece of scrap paper and keeps a different paper on each pile. When she is done, she brings them back to the counter. "There young man, I think this information will help you look good. Not that you have trouble in that department." She bats her eyes at him.

He looks at the notes. The cash payment property is just a mile from the farm office. "Loretta, just one other thing. I see these are stamped paid but there is no check number. Did Mr. Grant come in himself to pay these? I don't know why he didn't ask us to do it for him?" He slides the pile back to her. She looks at them and turns to a different ledger. A few moments go by as she is flipping pages.

She returns to the counter. "You were right. Mr. Johnson didn't come in, himself. He had his man, Albert Croner, pay them, in person, for the four years that he owned the property. Mr. Croner always paid in cash.

Matthew's mouth dropped open. "Albert Croner? You said Albert Croner has paid this in cash since 1935? And, every payment since then? You are sure, about this?"

Loretta smiles at Matthew, again. "I put the initials AC when I entered each payment. I also put in very small letters 'i c k' afterward. I know that it is Albert Croner because even though he is old enough to be my grandfather, he is always trying to sweet talk me to go out with him. Croner gives me the creeps – AC-ick! Like I'd ever even consider it. DOUBLE-ICK!!

   ***

The number of mourners have doubled! Helen thought to herself. *I didn't know that EL Dorado had this many residents!*

Once again, Joshua and his sister Carolyn insists that Helen rest for a few minutes each hour.

The Harricks have come to pay their respects. Anna and Henry leave Clara Beth with Frank and Judy back at Melinda's house. They arrive at three p.m. and must wait outside in line. On one of Helen's rests, she looks out the window at the line and sees Anna and Henry. She calls to her husband to go get them. When he brings them in, he brings them directly to Helen. "Why were you outside in line? You are family."

Henry says, "I told her that."

"We . . . I . . . didn't want to go past all the waiting people. I didn't know how long they were waiting or how close they are to you or your Papa." Anna explains.

Helen says, "Sometimes Anna, your humility just amazes me. I have lived with you for eight months and you proclaim to be Joshua's sister. Would I have Carolyn wait in line, outside?"

"No, I suppose not. But all those people in line . . ."

"Are not <u>my</u> family!" Helen finishes Anna's sentence for her. "I have never met anyone like you." She chuckles, and puts her arm around Anna's waist. "What am I going to do with you?"

"Henry asks me that all the time." Anna shrugs and puts her arm around her waist, also. "How are you holding up, Helen? Is there anything that I can do for you?"

"You are doing it, by being here. Thank you for coming. Have you seen your brother or father, yet?"

"No, Ma said they were on a fact-finding mission."

"They were and I am dying to find out what they have discovered. My 'rest time' is up. I must go relieve my Grand Mamá at the reception line.

Helen's eyes are constantly searching for Matthew who doesn't show up until almost 5 p.m. There are too many people always surrounding the family and they can't all get away at the same time. Matthew says that they should go back to the Johnson farmhouse for him to explain it all.

At 8 p.m. the last of the mourners were encouraged to leave and Helen was once again, allowed to say good-night to her papa, in private. After she bent to kiss him, the realization hit her that she will never be able to kiss her father, good-night, again. Tears quickly formed and Joshua was at her side. She tried hard to stop crying but it all crashed in on her. *"Papa, you will never hold me in your arms. I will never be able to call out 'Kisses' and you pretend to catch them in the air and place them on your cheek, again. You were my hero and my best friend. How will I survive without being able to talk with you?"*

She turns to her husband. "Joshua, I cannot take this pain! I don't want him to be gone. I don't want this to be our last good-night! I will never be able to hold his hand, again. I will never feel him near me, giving me strength, holding me up." Joshua is holding her tight, but has no words to comfort her. Her Grand Mamá steps in and Joshua lets her hold her next. Helen is simply inconsolable.

Mr. Kirby is just outside of the alcove, allowing the family to grieve as they must. Joshua goes to him and whispers something to him. Kirby turns and goes into his office. Joshua follows him. When they come out of the office, Joshua has some things in his hands. He goes to Helen.

"Darling, I have something for you." She looks down at the items in his hands. She is confused by them. Her sobs have lessened as she tries to concentrate on what he is trying to put in her hands.

"I don't understand. What are the scissors and envelope for, Joshua?" Her body is still breathing in sobs like an infant does, after a good cry.

Joshua explains. "It isn't fair that you feel that your Papa will not be with you. He is all around you, and will never leave you. But, if you want just a part of him to always be with you, let's cut off a few curls of his hair, and put it in the envelope for now. Later I will buy you a beautiful locket for his golden locks, so that you can wear it next to your heart, forever. Do you want me to do this for you?" She is just staring at her husband. She lets him take the scissors back from her. He approaches Grant's casket and reaches for the side toward the lid. "I will cut a few curls off this side and no one will notice during tomorrow's services. I will cut an extra curl for you, also, Grand Mamá." He clips very carefully, as he holds the envelope under the scissors to catch the cut hairs. His eyes begin to tear as he whispers. "Oh, Grant, you were such a good person and father. Please always watch over your Juliet Helen." He says as a soft prayer to the deceased.

"There, that should do it." He turns back to his bride and her grandmother to see their eyes are still brimming with tears but smiles are on their lips.

"That is the sweetest most thoughtful gesture, any man has ever done, Joshua. My great-granddaughter picked one of the best! *IF,* I wasn't sure about your feelings for her, this would have cleared up any doubts." Carolyn Lewis Johnson moves to him and kisses him on his cheek. "She is in the best hands in the country, and I will testify to that, my boy. I will swear to it on a very tall stack of bibles."

***

The Masters' clan, the Harrick's, and the Collin's all come back to the Johnson Farmhouse after the wake. Matilda and Melinda and Anna make everyone some sandwiches and a fresh pot of coffee is brewed.

Joshua could tell that there was some news from the trip to the Assessor's Office. Matthew did not have his poker face on, today. As everyone finishes the sandwiches and are now on Anna's pies, Joshua says, "Matthew, what is going on? Did we catch a break, finally?"

"Pa and I think so. We checked out all the addresses that we were given from the assessor. None of the farms had a building that could be used by Grant as the headache house, except for the one property that he paid the taxes in cash. We went to the address given to us. It was only a mile down from the Farm Office but a house is far off on a small dirt road. Neither Pa nor I ever noticed it behind all the trees that line the road. We looked in all the windows of the small two-bedroom home, and it looks like it is STILL lived in. We waited around for someone to come home but no one showed up. It doesn't matter, though, we know who is staying there."

He was playing with the last piece of the pie but looked up

at everyone. He was smiling. "Albert Croner has been paying the tax bill since 1935. Even though we fired the creep when we took over, he stayed on to take care of Grant. We need to look at the ledgers, again, to find some regular withdrawals that would prove he was STILL on Grant's payroll."

Helen looks at Matthew. "The name doesn't sound familiar. Do I know this guy?"

Melinda jumps in, "If you don't, count yourself blessed. He is a grabby low life scum! When he wasn't yelling at the women in the fields, he was putting his sweating hands on us. I hit him in the face with a tomato, once. He never bothered me after that."

"And this is the man that Papa had to care for him? Something doesn't seem right about this."

Judd speaks up. "He didn't treat women with an ounce of respect but he was a yes-man to anyone with money. I expect he enjoyed earning a check playing a nurse maid. He did not like manual labor, that was for sure!"

Matthew says. "Bet he is sorry now. No Grant to leech off. I wonder if he knew what Grant was suffering from. Or, if he knew it was a short-term arrangement? If he just found out, would he get mad enough to kill him? This is what we need to figure out and quickly!"

TWENTY-ONE

An Excerpt from Elizabeth Lewis's Journal
Monday, November 8, 1880 in Lawrence, Kansas

The newspapers were reporting the number of Cheyenne deaths, in Nebraska, daily. My son, the Major, has barely had a chance to get there to make a difference when General Crook decided to remove Wessells from Fort Robinson. Our Will arrived by stagecoach by January 18th.

He had immediately found the chase for the escapees hopeless. More than half were already dead. Some killed in battle but more died from their own hand or doing because they were determined to choose their manner of death if they couldn't choose their manner of living.

One young brave, called Mantotohpa was separated from his warrior mother Nokomis but he was determined to save his little sister. When he heard my Will's troops nearby he told the little girl to lie down in a valley and he covered her with leaves and twigs. He had his mother's rifle and he walked a few yards from her and called out to Will in his native tongue.

Will wrote that he tried to motion to the young brave just barely over the age of fifteen or sixteen to surrender. The boy raised the rifle, instead, took aim and fired. He shot a private's horse, but was riddled with bullets within moments. He let out a loud war cry with his dying breath. It wasn't until the next day that the troops found the girl almost frozen to death, still in her hiding place.

The little girl, Ayita was somewhere between seven and nine years old and spoke a few words of English. She wasn't afraid of Will for some reason and took to him. He gave her some candy and hard tack and she wanted to follow him around from then on. She rode on his horse all the way back to Fort Robinson which took two days' time.

When they arrived at the Fort, the doctor treated her for frost bite. William brought her hot soup and cooked fresh meat. He fed her himself and she ate herself to sleep, right at the table.

When Will lifted her off the table to put her to her cot, she whispered something to him that is almost too good to be true.

She told Will that he was a good brave and looked just like a boy a little older than herself that was taken from the place of the great round-up of horses and cattle. She said his name was Joshua in the white man's tongue but that they changed it to Harkahome for the trip to their homeland.

When Will asked why he was taken, she said that a white man tried to kill her other brother and Harkahome pushed the gun away and saved Degotoga's life. Their father repaid the debt by taking Harkahome with them, instead of killing him.

Of all the investigations and interviews with the survivors of Oberlin, how did this stay a secret?

When Ayita's mother was found the next week, she was questioned and admitted that a young boy, Harkahome, was taken from the village. She claimed to not know his white man's name.

Will pleaded with General Crook to follow Little Wolf's trail to see if his nephew was alive. He knew he had to find the little boy or if he didn't, he had to find justice for Joshua!!

An excerpt from the Letters of Major William Lewis

March 10th, 1879

Dearest Julia,

My dearest Cousin, I received your letter from January at Fort Robinson just last week. I am much relieved that you are still in Lawrence with Mother. She has repeatedly said that she relies on you for so much.

In your letter, I think that you said that you wish for my safe and swift return to you. Such wonderful words to hear. I would have liked to have read that letter again and again but a mishap occurred and the letter became coffee laden and no longer readable. I was a grown man with tears in my eyes at the loss. The private that spilled the coffee was docked a day's pay and I do not regret it in the least.

The real sad news is that my return is not yet to be. As you know, there is word that my nephew Joshua may still be alive and held captive with Little Wolf's tribe. Fifty-eight of the Cheyenne survivors have been permitted to live at the Pine Ridge Reservation in South Dakota. I must go to see if my nephew is with the tribe. Or, if they know if he has been taken elsewhere, or GOD FORBID, if he perished in the journey. If he is not with them, I am permitted to pursue the rest of Little Wolf's tribe to their destination in Montana. I do not know how long any of this will take. Winter is still heavy in these parts, and travel will be slow.

I do not wish to burden you any further by waiting for me to arrive in Lawrence. You have done more than I had hoped by being Mother's constant companion during my absence. I absolve you of any further obligation to stay on. Your home is in El Dorado, and I will come to you there as soon as it is possible to do so.

Dearest cousin, this release does not in any way lessen what I am feeling for you. I am forever your Will, if you will have me. This is so bold as we have not set eyes upon each other in over three years. Mother has told me that you have grown even more beautiful and my heart aches for my eyes to behold you once again.

I do not know when I will be able to get another letter from you. (Curse that Private!) You may try to get one to me through the Pine River Indian Agency, since that is my first destination.

Until then my Dearest Cousin, continue to pray for my success in finding Joshua unharmed, and our safe and swift return to Kansas.

I cannot close this letter until I share another warming memory. Our second kiss, do you recall the circumstances? I remember the peach dress that you were wearing at that dance as it is branded in my memory, as well as my heart. I remember the small peach colored roses that you had in your dark, long lovely hair that was pinned up high upon your head. You had all the boys waiting to dance with you and though you were surrounded by suitors, you looked across the room to me and when our eyes met, you nodded. That affirmation gave my feet the courage to walk past the boys with their forlorn eyes and take you by the hand without saying a word and lead you onto the dance floor. I think we were fifteen or sixteen at the time and during the dance you leaned in to thank me - I _thought_ - but you kissed my cheek instead. I can almost still feel the warmth of your lips. I remember the blush that spread up your lovely neck after that kiss and how you shyly looked around the room to see if anyone had seen. I remember the smell of your Rosewater perfume, and it was magnificent! I've hardly passed a rose without thinking of you and that second kiss. And now I am warm from reliving it all, once again!

I will try to share a warming memory of how we were together, each time I can sit down to write to you. I want to prove to you that I am forever your servant and a slave to those memories.

Yours very truly,
Major Wm. Lewis

TWENTY-TWO

November 9th, 1939
Thursday in EL Dorado, Kansas

The dreaded day has dawned. Helen must bury her father. *How will I go on?* As if the heavens are crying, there is a light rain falling and it is predicted to fall most of the morning.

At ten a.m., the families and friends all gather at the Kirby Funeral Home. Outside, there is a long line of black umbrellas keeping hundreds of mourners dry. Helen cannot believe the crowd. Mr. Kirby in his many years of experience, knew to put just two hours down for the mourners' final good-byes but to make the Church services an hour and a half after that. He knew that it would take that long for the rest of those in line to make their way in. Just before noon, he makes his announcement. "Ladies and Gentleman. On behalf of the family of Mr. Grant Johnson, we thank you for attending these services. After everyone has said their good-byes, please exit and let the family have their last private moments. There will be a short service at The EL Dorado 1st Congregational Church at 1:30 this afternoon followed by a procession to the EL Dorado Christian Cemetery. You may join us, and the family thanks you. There will be a Mourners potluck, thanks to the wonderful services of the Ladies of the Mourner's Society, in the basement of the church, immediately following the cemetery as a thank you for your attendance."

That begins the silent single file procession passed the casket and out. Helen and Joshua are sitting in the front row on the loveseat. Grand Mamá Carolyn was in a high back cushioned seat, looking blankly ahead. A steady silent flow of tears fell from her eyes, even though she sat as straight and tall as the chair with no emotion showing on her face. Helen's heart was breaking watching her great-grandmother go through yet another loss. *I cannot believe how she can hold up after going through this so many times. Each one of these losses feels like a stab through the heart. How can one keep going?*

The mourner procession was finally over and the door is closed for the family to have their private goodbye. This is the moment that Helen has dreaded for days. She leans against Joshua and whispers, "How can I say goodbye?"

He whispers back. "Don't. Tell him *'I will see you later, papa.'* You do believe that he and your mother are together and waiting for you, don't you?" He waits for her answer. When she doesn't respond, he puts his hand over hers. "Helen, you do believe that, don't you?"

"Right now, Joshua, I do not know what I believe." She says with a sob in her throat.

"Helen, I believe <u>that</u> is as true as our love. Can you take my word for it then?" She nods, slowly. The first of the family to say their goodbyes is Matilda held up by Sullivan. She does not hold back her sorrow and wails loudly.

Grand Mamá leaves her chair and crosses to Matilda and puts her hand on her shoulder and whispers something in her ear. Carolyn Johnson was taller than the five-foot sixty-plus-year old black woman and had to bend over slightly. She pats her back a few times and Matilda suddenly turns around and places her arms around the other woman's waist and cries into her bosom. The elegant woman with the Gibson girl hairstyle allows Matilda time to calm down, stroking her hair. "Mattie, we have to continue on, now. Chin up, Master Grant wouldn't want you to carry on so in front of his Juliet Helen. Dry your eyes, please. Sullivan, can you take her?"

Sullivan has been quietly crying but he steps forward and takes his mother's arms from around Gram Carolyn's waist. "Maw, we have to let the others say goodbye. Come on, Maw." He leads her to the back of the room. The Masters family had said their goodbyes and are at the back of the room. Judy Masters changes sides with Judd so that she can hold and hug Matilda. The two women turn towards the front, but Judy is still holding onto Matilda's hand.

Susan and her Matthew pass the casket now. Susan bends down and gives Grant a kiss on the cheek. "Say hi to Auntie for me." Then she pats his hands and turns to her husband in tears. Matthew holds her a moment while she silently cries into his chest. He urges her to move forward and as she does so she pulls away from him and dabs her eyes. Then, they go to the back of the room.

Doctor Benjamin Johnson and his wife Annabelle come forward. Doc is the original Grant's cousin. Carolyn's father-in-law had three younger half-siblings. They were Gloria, Benjamin(Sr.) and George, all of whom had sons. They stand a moment over the casket. Doc reaches in and pats Grant's shoulder a few times and they move to the rear. Sheriff Sam Johnson, Doc's son, comes forward. He quickly does the same action as his father. Estelle and Miller Johnson, a nephew to the Doc, moves up to pay their respects. Mark Collins, with his wife Melinda pushes his grandmother, Gloria, who is one of the original four siblings, in a wheel chair. She is ninety-eight-years old. She is emotionless as she says her small prayer in front of the casket. Again, Gram Carolyn is on her feet. She walks over to her husband's aunt and gives her a kiss on the cheek before Mark takes her to the back of the room. Twenty-something more people with the Johnson surname come up and quickly retreat to the rear.

Once they are all done, Gram Carolyn approaches her grandson Grant. She bends to kiss his forehead and pats his hands, and says, "See you later. Say hi to your Grandfather for me, tell him I miss him most of all." She wipes a single tear then kisses him again.

Now the only one left to pass the casket is Helen and her husband. Joshua helps her stand and has his arm around her waist. They are at the casket in just a few steps. Helen reaches for her father's cheek and strokes it. "Papa, remember when you let me shave you? You were so brave, even then. How you must have suffered and yet refused to show us your pain. How brave to have spared us all that! I hope that I can be but a shadow of the great person that you were, Papa. *I already miss you so much! But now, I must be brave like you and carry this pain so that the world never sees it.*" She bends down and kisses his cold lips. When she stands back up she turns to Joshua. He has his hand on Grant's shoulder and tears are running down his face. "There, there, Joshua. We will see him again." She says as a small smile changes just the corners of her mouth. "I do believe." She says simply.

As they file back, Mr. Kirby steps forward to close the casket. He has handed out gloves for the Pall bearers to wear. He announces, "Gentlemen, please come forward and take your places." Doc, the Sheriff, Miller, Mark Collins and two other Johnson cousins surround the casket and guide it to the awaiting hearse.

The rest of the afternoon slowly ticks away for Helen. Now that her father is out of sight, she feels that it is over. The service at the church and the lowering of the casket into the ground at the cemetery were just motions without meaning.

They attend the luncheon surrounded by well-wishers but Helen is in a daze. At the end of the luncheon, Gram Carolyn stands in front and announces, "We cannot thank you enough for this show of love, respect, and support that you have shown our family. I know that this has been an exhausting emotional event for myself as well as Juliet Helen. We will take our leave now. But, please stay as long, as you wish and again, thank you." She turns to Helen. "We can leave now. I think you need a long nap, my dear. You look drained." She helps her to her feet and with Joshua on her other side, the three go home.

Helen and Grand Mamá rest for a few hours. At 5:30, the doorbell rings and it is Judy, Anna and Melinda with trays and platters of hot food, once again, for the grieving household.

TWENTY-THREE

An Excerpt from Elizabeth Lewis's Journal Tuesday
November 9, 1880 in Lawrence, Kansas

In 1879, my son Major Will was off to find my grandson Joshua Nathaniel. My heart was so hopeful for his success but sick with worry at the same time. Will got permission to take the little girl, Ayita, and her mother, Nokomis, as guides and translators to the Pine River Indian Reservation. The Squaw agreed to it, hoping to be reunited with her husband, Kanuna and Ayita's brother Degotoga.

The squaw and her daughter were permitted a horse to ride and a gun to carry for their own protection. Nokomis, felt greatly honored by this show of respect (only warrior women rode horses) and of trust (that she would not use the gun on him).

Even on horseback, the winter weather made the going burdensome and of great peril. It took almost a full month for them to reach the Dakota territory. Ayita would ride behind Will as often as her mother would allow. Will took his time traveling and took advantage of the hours by trying to learn some of the Cheyenne language. He knew a little French and was surprised how much of the language had telltale French roots. Even the name of the people, Cheyenne, came from the French word 'chein' which means dog. This tribe was called Dog soldiers by the Apache and they soon became known as the Cheyenne.

It was with great sadness that I had to say goodbye to my guest Julia Johnson. She felt that she needed to go home for a little while. She promised to return in a month or so, and to insure it she took Carolyn to EL Dorado with her. Carolyn is just fourteen years old and begged and begged to go for the outing. I was against it since she would have to miss school. Julia promised to continue Carolyn's lessons and very determined to do so. She made an appointment with the head mistress at Carolyn's school so that she can get all necessary books and

110

goals for the month so that when Carolyn comes back she will not be behind in her work.

True to her word, five weeks later, Julia brought Carolyn home to me. The change in my youngest daughter was amazing. Though, already, tall for her age when she returned she stood taller and was far less silly than when she left. All she could talk about was how grand Julia's older brother was to her. The girl was thoroughly smitten and did not try to hide it. She and Grant have since, corresponded regularly.

As has Julia, and her Will.

An excerpt from the letters of Julia Johnson ,

April 2, 1879

Dearest Will,

Dearest Cousin, I hope this letter finds you on your search for your nephew. I also hope that you keep this missive away from Privates with coffee!

I wanted to let you know that I did go home as you said I should but I did not stay but a few weeks and I was off back to Lawrence. I had taken your sister, Carolyn, with me and we got very close on the trip, though she is seven years my junior. I, even, worked with her on her lessons, as I promised.

It was amazing to see the change in her when we got to El Dorado. She immediately had puppy dog eyes for my brother, Grant, who is ten years her senior. He had little time for her but she managed to endear herself to him with short work. I have a suspicion that there are substantial feelings going both ways. Since we've arrived in Lawrence, she has received three letters from him, and he was as bad at writing letters as you were.

I am thrilled that you are now very, very good at writing letters. I have reread your last letter almost every night (I have no-coffee-spilling-Privates). I am waiting ever so _impatiently_ for the next one to arrive. Though your circumstances for writing must be very challenging, I hope that you will be able to do so as soon as possible.

In the meantime, I wait beside your Mother, missing you and worrying about you. I will be here in Lawrence, when you come home, for I feel as though it has always been my home.

The only thing that is missing is you, my Will. My dearest, dearest cousin. I cannot wait to make memories together, once again.

Can I correct one of your memories? You said that the snowball fight was our first kiss and the dance was the second but you are dead wrong, my darling. How do you not remember our true first kiss? I am almost disappointed in you for forgetting it. That first kiss changed my life forever and you do not speak of it!

It was right after Ian's wedding. Your mother was in bed about to give birth to Chilly. Do you recall it now? I will not say anymore. You must come up with the rest of the memory or maybe you do not think of me in as high a regard as you claim to do. I am telling you, our real first kiss altered me in a way that no man will ever be able to have that effect on me again! My eyes saw you for the first time as the one for me. What a kiss!

Come home to Lawrence, dearest cousin, and let me show you what that kiss did for me. Now who is being so bold?

Yours very truly,
Julia

TWENTY-FOUR

November 10th, 1939
Friday in EL Dorado, Kansas

Another dreaded day's sunlight wakes Helen from her fitful sleep. Joshua's Preliminary Hearing is later this morning. She turns to look at him. *What if they revoke his bond? What if he is found guilty? This may be the last time I wake up next to the father of my baby! What will become of him, of us, of me?* She begins to silently cry as she moves into his arms. He awakens and automatically takes her in and kisses her. He hasn't opened his eyes but his body moves in practiced loving motions. She is glad that he doesn't look at her. She wants this to be a sacred union, not spoiled by her tears. As he is about to finish, he says, "Always, my Helen, I will love you, always."

She smiles and adds, breathlessly, "as I do you, Joshua, always." She feels so much love for this man that she can hardly take it in. *How was I so stupid as to leave him for even a minute?*

As they slowly uncouple, Joshua's eyes open and he reaches to stroke her face. He feels her wet hair from her tears. "No crying, Helen. We will be just fine. I am not going anywhere. I am innocent and we will find a way to prove that, I am sure of it."

"If only you can promise that." She kisses his cheek, wipes her tears away and starts to rise. "We have a busy day, today. We must get started. It's my time to be brave like Papa." She sighs loudly and sits up on her side of the bed. "Do you know what suit you want to wear?"

"Anna only packed three and I have worn them all this week. You pick. Then it will be my lucky one."

She turns to look at him. "I don't feel like your lucky charm. You wouldn't be charged with my father's murder if you hadn't met me or followed me to EL Dorado."

"But you wouldn't be carrying my child, either. I choose to

114

consider myself a lucky man. Just like the Colonel always said
he was. That didn't mean troubles didn't find their way to him.
He buried his only son, raised his two young grandchildren,
buried the love of his life then suffered with dementia. But he
always said that he was the luckiest man alive because he had
found his true love. 'And they lived happily ever after' is what
he always said, remember?" He reaches for her, again. She
lets him take her into his arms again. "Luckiest man, alive."
He repeats and he kisses her gently on the lips. "I do believe."
He adds simply.

***

Mr. Miles Curtis, the Defense Attorney recommended by
the family law firm of Dewey and Howe had come to the estate
last night, after dinner to discuss the case. He was surprised
at all that they had dug up regarding the 'headache house' and
Albert Croner. At eight a.m., he is at the front door to take
Joshua and Helen to court. Eddie is talking to him when Helen
and Joshua come down the stairs.

Mr. Miles looked to the couple, "Joshua, my boy, how are
you today?"

"Nervous. What is the worst that can happen to me today?
Can they put me back in jail?"

"Absolutely not! This is no more than an evidentiary
proceeding. They will ask for a plea, of course, but not much
else."

Eddie interrupts. "Mr. Miles, please make sure that you
get us as much time as possible between now and the trial to
come up with solid evidence against the other suspect. We are
going to follow him around, which might take some time."

"And I have to build my case to refute all the evidence
against my client. I will need to know the intimate details of
your personal and business finances. I will come over early
next week, or would it be easier if I came to Lawrence for a
financial conference?"

Helen answers, "You mean we can go back home before the
trial?" She squeezes Joshua's hand.

"My girl, I will insist that the judge allows it. Your

husband is an important man in Lawrence and the family business needs its leader back at the helm. That's what I am going to tell him, anyway." He smiles at her. "I understand that congratulations are in order. You are glowing. Have you had morning sickness so far?"

"Thank you and no sir, I have been lucky. No sickness at all" She squeezes her husband's hand again.

"We should get going. Court is at nine sharp and you do not want to make the judge mad by being late." He picks up his briefcase and heads to the door. Joshua and Helen follow him. "We should be home by lunchtime, I for one, always work up an appetite when I am in court."

Helen looks to Eddie. "Have Matilda start on a huge lunch for us, please." She calls out to the attorney. "Mr. Miles?" He turns with his hand on the doorknob. "What is your favorite lunch? Fried chicken or soup or a roast beef sandwich? Name it and they will have it ready when we return."

"My girl, one can never go wrong with fried chicken! Now my mouth is watering, let's get there quick so we can get back! Oh, Boy Howdy! Fried Chicken!" He is saying as he is walking out the door.

Helen smiles at Eddie, then shrugs. "I like him, don't you? Tell Mattie to start frying!" She walks out after him.

Joshua is following her out when his sister Carolyn calls after him. "Wait, Joshua. I want to give you a hug for good luck!" He stops and Helen stops also.

Joshua says, "You can hug me Carolyn but my luck is coming with me." Helen glows from the comment.

***

It is a little after the noon hour and Eddie, Matthew and Susan are once again pouring over the books looking for any unexplained regular payout that would compensate Croner for his services. The fried chicken smell was making their mouths water and their stomachs rumble. "I hope they get home soon. I may not be able to take this much longer." Matthew gripes.

Susan elbows him. "That's my husband, always hungry!"

She stands to mess up his hair. He moves out of her way just in time for Eddie to reach him and get the job done.

"Susan, that's because he is just a growing boy, don't you know?" Eddie laughs.

"Hey, I am going to be twenty any day now!"

"Not any day, Matthew, tomorrow." Susan corrects him.

"I won't make it unless they get here so that lunch is served. I am about to starve to death."

Before anyone can answer him, Carolyn yells from the front parlor, "Thank God, they are home!"

Everyone rushes to greet them. Carolyn opens the door and runs to her brother. "Well, how did it go? How long do we have until your trial? Did anything come out that we didn't know about?" She rushes all the important questions out to him but does not give him a moment to answer any of them.

"Carolyn, calm down. Let's get inside. Helen is exhausted. Mr. Miles, I smell your fried chicken. I think you earned it, sir."

"Oh, boy howdy! I love fried chicken. I will only stay for a bit. I need to work on our strategy. How they came up with all those ridiculous notions!" He suddenly stops in his tracks. "Joshua, Helen, please introduce me to this elegant young lady." He is looking directly at Grand Mamá.

Helen does the honors. "Mr. Miles Curtis, this is my Great Grand Mamá, Carolyn Lewis Johnson. Grand Mamá, this is Joshua's attorney -Mr. Miles Curtis."

Grand Mamá holds out her hand for him to shake it but he takes it to his lips instead. "Ma-am, the pleasure is all mine. How could someone so young be this grown woman's Great Grand Mamá?"

Gram Carolyn smiles her elegant smile and says, "Poppy Cock, Mr. Miles Curtis! You are the spitting image of your father and he was just as big a flirt as I see you are." She then gives him a little swat on the shoulder with the hand he was just kissing. "That doesn't mean I want you to stop, mind you. I just thought that you should know that you don't fool me one bit. I swear, exactly like your flirting father. How is your mom, by the way?"

"Mama is doing just fine and told me to give you her

regards, if I saw you." He winks at her.

They are now seating themselves at the dining room table. Grand Mamá is at the head. On one side of her is her namesake with her husband beside her. On the other side is Helen with her husband beside her. Susan is at the opposite head of the table and has Matthew on her right and Mr. Miles on her left.

Joshua's sister Carolyn says, "Enough of the niceties, fill us in on the courtroom. What do they have on Joshua besides the gun and the insurance policy?"

The attorney says, "they have the sworn statement from a black man named Sullivan, that Joshua made those threats."

There is a clatter at the sideboard, where Sullivan has almost dropped a tray of coffee cups. "Beg, your pardon, sir. I didn't swear to anything. They asked me if anyone was mad at Master Grant and I said that you were. I didn't mean you no harm. Honest, Mister Joshua." He looks to the attorney. "Can I say it did not happen? Can we say that I was overcome with grief over Master Grant's death? Would they believe me? Can I refuse to testify?"

"Not to worry, my dear man. I can get you on the stand and you will say just that. You were overcome with emotion and exaggerated the events, which you are known to do. I do not think that your testimony will be damning to the defendant." He turns to Joshua, "but this business of the insurance will be damning unless we prove either of two things. One – that you have more than enough and have no need for the excess that it will give you. Two – there is reasonable doubt that someone else is responsible for the murder."

Then he looks from Matthew to Eddie. "That's where you two gentlemen come in. I asked for the maximum time, sixty days, but I was only granted a few weeks. The trial is set for December 4th. You are planning on trailing this Croner fella, then?"

Eddie speaks up. "We have devised a schedule to have an around-the-clock-watch on the house until we spot Croner then we will try to keep a tail on him. We have enlisted a few of our friends from a detective agency we use in Lawrence. They are very good at blending into a crowd and have ham radios in their cars to talk with each other."

Matthew fidgets. "I want in on the tracking!"

Eddie shakes his head no. "Matthew, you have your classes to attend. Also, you mentioned that Croner knows you and has always had a problem with you. I think once we have his whereabouts down. We will send you in to confront him."

Grand Mamá says, "I feel like we are in a Sam Spade Novel!" She smiles. "If this wasn't so serious, I'd be excited."

TWENTY-FIVE

An Excerpt from Elizabeth Lewis's Journal
Wednesday, November 10, 1880 in Lawrence, Kansas

The Pine River Indian Reservation had been getting more and more Cheyenne refugees coming in by the day. Julia's letter was waiting for Will but neither Nokomis' family nor our Joshua Nathaniel were there.

With my son's influence, the Southern Cheyenne had permission to continue up to their ancestral home in Montana. This is all that they wanted in the first place! Of the three hundred and fifty-three souls that left the Darlington Agency, chased afoot, starved for food, captured, tortured, escaped again, hunted down again, there were only one hundred fourteen survivors that made it this far north. And none of them were with my grandson!

The final leg of the journey was only a few hundred miles. Out of his own money, Will bought several wagons and horses to carry the tired, young, old and infirm. He made a pact with them. He would transport them to Montana, where the Yellowstone and the Tongue Rivers meet. This is their ancestral homeland, and there is a fort there, Fort Keogh.

The pact with them was that if his nephew finds his way there, they would contact the Fort and get a message to him. Of course, they would have to surrender any remaining braves responsible for the settler massacre. He would escort them back to Kansas to stand trial. Another dangerous mission.

Julia has remained with us since she came back from El Dorado. She was a delight, and helps with all the farm activities and aids the younger children with their school work. Charles, or Chilly as we've always called him is thirteen and like Will in school, he needs help with his numbers and letters on occasion. Will doesn't seem to have a problem with letters any longer, much to the pleasure of his Julia.

120

An Excerpt from the letters of Major William Lewis

April 17, 1879

My Dearest Julia,

Dearest Cousin, I am so very thankful to have had your letter waiting for me at the Pine River Agency. Finally, something hopeful to warm me from the inside out, barring all Privates at a twenty-pace distance.

After such a long solitary ride, out here with just Nokomis and Ayita for conversation, your letter is a breath of fresh air. Ayita sends her best wishes to you. I described your long dark hair and your soulful brown eyes and your small stature to her and told her how we grew up together. I had to explain the word 'cousin' to her but I am not sure that she understands the concept. Her people do not assign family placement outside of father, mother, daughter and son. All live together as brothers and sisters and all grandmothers are grandmothers to all.

Nokomis is very quiet compared to her daughter. I know that she speaks just a little English but understands more than she lets on. If Ayita rode on my horse for any length of time, Nokomis would have Ayita go over all that we discussed. I have been making the effort to learn some of the language, and it's made the Cheyenne treat me differently than they have the other white men.

Ayita has given me a Cheyenne/French name that means roughly TOO TALL. My name is Navoualevé. Now that we are heading out for Montana, I have thirty-three braves, and forty-three squaws and too many children to keep still to count, all calling me this. Sometimes they shorten it to just Alevé. I rather like the sound of it in their tongue which does not make it sound French-y at all.

I expect to have all the provisions arrive for our departure within the week for the trip to Montana. I am trying to get wagons and horses for them as well as food supplies and guns. We have already seen buffalo and now the Cheyenne can hunt for their own food and not rely on the promises of their White Father. Promises never kept. When the Cheyenne were promised food and safe shelter at the Darlington Agency they were almost one thousand People strong. They had buried hundreds in shallow graves because of the shallow promises from our government. I am escorting just a few more than one hundred Cheyenne to Montana. All those souls lost to promises never kept.

Now, I must respond to your accusation of my not knowing the order of the kisses. I do so much know the order. I kissed _you_ when I was seven years old, and you slapped me, and I had to write notes of apology to you and your mother for my impolite, unrequested, show of affection. I remember the joy that I felt, when I heard that you were moving to Lawrence that I was overcome with emotion. I was so taken by you from the first time I saw you. That first sighting was just before Grandfather's wedding. Your mother came to Lawrence to attend your Grandmother's marriage to him. By the time of Ian's wedding, she had decided to move to Lawrence with you and Grant. You acted as though living in Lawrence wasn't a big deal but it meant everything to me. As it does now.

So, the count started. I kissed you at seven, and got slapped. You kissed me at fourteen or fifteen after the snowball fall. You kissed me a second time when I took you out on the dance floor and age fifteen or sixteen. Our first kiss _together_ was the following Christmas. My sister-in-law Lydia had a big Christmas party at the City Hotel and she put up mistletoe in several doorways. We danced a few songs together then you took me to the doorway, stood under the beam and pointed up to the mistletoe. I remember that my mouth fell open at the thought, that you were giving me permission to kiss you. I remember shaking as I took your face into my hands and bent slowly place my lips upon yours. I remember that I tried to pull away from your soft lips when your hands sought my face and held me there. Then nine-year-old Chilly and eight-year-old Joshua Nathaniel saw us, and made such a fuss that I wanted to kill them both.

So, Dearest Cousin, I do remember which kiss was which for they were all as important to me as my first steps, or my first day of school or my graduation day. They were all life changing *moments because when each of those kisses happened, my life was never, EVER the same again.*

I would like to make plans for the next set of very important kisses but I do not want to make any promises that my current obligations will prevent me from keeping. All that I can promise is that there are kisses in our future and that if you will have me, we will live happily ever after. That is my solemn vow. If you promise, to be at my side, making each day special with your beautiful smile, and those dark, dark eyes that give me such comfort to look in, I will love you for all the rest of my days. If you will have me, I am your Will.

Yours Very Truly,
Major William Lewis

TWENTY-SIX

November 11th, 1939
Saturday in EL Dorado, Kansas

Judd and Judy are up at their usual early hour. Breakfast has already been served and cleaned. The Harrick's: Anna, Henry, Clara Beth and Frank are still in town. The two women are baking in Melinda's roomy kitchen. They are baking bread and a very special cake for Matthew. The pans are finally in the oven, and Anna takes Clara Beth to the potty.

Judy sighs and says. "I feel so old. My baby boy is twenty already! How the times flies. I can still see him taking his first steps. Now he is married with a little one of his own."

"Oh, Ma, you don't look old at all, I am the one with all the wrinkles for being in the sun all those years." Now Judd sighs. "I don't know how we would have survived if Grant hadn't given us jobs, out of pity." He muses.

"Yes, but within a year, you proved yourself to him and he put you in charge of everything."

"I took great pride in that until I just found out that Grant was desperate. Keeping Croner on, what was he thinking? We explained why we let him go, but Grant kept him on."

"Judd, he would not have left his business that he built up by hand if you were not capable. As for Croner, well . . ." She turns to look at her husband. "He probably felt sorry for the guy because he bought his property from him and bulldozed his house, remember? You told me that story, yourself."

"I suppose. What kind of cake are you baking for Matthew? Red velvet is his favorite, you know." He winks at his wife.

Judd Andrew Masters, red velvet is <u>your</u> favorite cake. German chocolate is Matthew's. You are so bad!" She walks over to him and swats him with the towel from around her apron.

Melinda walks into the kitchen. "Ma, why are you hitting my father?" She walks over to her mother and gives her a kiss on the cheek. "You never hit us but you don't seem to have a problem hitting grown men! Do you remember that time Frank picked you up and when he put you down you beat him with a wooden spoon?" They all could picture it like it was yesterday.

Clara Beth and her mother, Anna, come back into the kitchen. The little one runs to her grandfather's lap and climbs up uninvited and unaided. She sits down and puts her hands under her chin just like her grandpa is doing above her. Judd pretends not to notice that she is in his lap. He moves his hand from his chin, slowly. Clara Beth is busy smiling at the grown-ups while she continues her imitation. Judd reaches down and begins to tickle her. She scrunches up to his touch and giggles loudly. "You little dickens, didn't you think that I noticed you there?"

Her giggles fill the kitchen and she cannot answer him. Finally, she gets tired of being tickled and squirms off his lap. She runs to her father, "Dada, Grandpa tickles!" She says as if she is mad.

"Well, did you ask for permission to climb up?" She shrugs her shoulders, understanding that she isn't getting sympathy from this grownup.

Henry looks to Judy, "Ma, what time are we headed to Matthew's? We wanted to go over to Helen and Joshua's for a spell."

"Whatever you do, don't mention that it's Matthew's birthday. He is most likely there, working on the case. Susan said that he is sure the answer is in the household books. I usually have Katie Ann but today she is by Susan's mom. Susan wants us to bring everything to her house at about six o'clock. I don't know why she is trying to surprise him."

"Maybe, we shouldn't go over there, then." Anna says. "I am sure that Susan has invited Helen, Carolyn and their menfolk."

Judy says, "I hope that she extended the invitation to Carolyn Johnson. They all need a break from mourning and worry."

Henry says, "Why don't I call Joshua, instead, then I could mention extending the invitation to Grand Mamá Carolyn without Matthew to hear."

***

At six o'clock, the Masters family bring a huge supper to Matthew's bungalow. Judy has a key to the house and they enter through the kitchen and begin to set up and decorate. Henry and Judd take the cars to the block behind the house to park.

Matthew expects to pick up Katie Ann then spend a quiet evening at home. The first quiet one in several days because of the wake and the investigation. Susan will ask Matthew to stop at the A & P store on the other side of town, which will give the Johnson household and Susan's Mother a chance to come to the house to surprise him.

Everyone has their cars on the block behind the house and they are in their hiding place in the bungalow. Susan is holding Katie Ann and Matthew has his arms laden with groceries as they make their way from the car in the dusky lighting of early winter. Susan leads the way but Matthew is right behind her. With her key in the door she says, "Put the groceries on the table, Matthew and I will turn on the lamp."

"Surprise!!!" Everyone yells as soon as the light is lit. Matthew has just put the bags down and grips his chest.

"I am an old man, now. I cannot take surprises like this," he laughs.

"Matthew, you knew?" Susan looks disappointed. "We put so much into this."

"Since when do you want to go to the A & P with Katie Ann in tow? You would have gone to the store before picking up Katie! That made me suspicious, to say the least. Thank you for trying, Susan." He bends down and gives her a little peck on the cheek. He looks up and says, "Henry, brother, good to see you." Now he is off among the guests having a good visit.

Later, Susan, Melinda and Anna are in the kitchen washing up some of the dishes from dinner before serving the cake. Susan was talking about her frustration in not finding the link between Croner and Grant. "There has to be a pay-out somewhere."

"I agree, Croner wouldn't spend a minute with Grant, without being paid."

"Well, I have yet to find it in the household books." They are done with the dishes, for now and go out to the kitchen table area.

Anna asks, "I have never handled accounts but have you looked in the Farm books, too? I know Pa has been doing them for years but how does the money go from the farm account to the house account? Grant surely makes a profit, maybe some of it doesn't make it to the household account because it goes to Croner? Or maybe, he has called the expense something else, like a store or business account that doesn't exist."

Melinda says. "Matthew? Come here a second. Pa?" Both men look at the young ladies. Melinda repeats what Anna said. "I think we should compare the farm books, too. I can help, I have off tomorrow and the afternoons, you know that I am good with numbers, also."

Matthew looks at his older sister, "I wouldn't want to tax you, in your condition, sis."

"I am just fine, Matthew, I can look at ledgers and accounts. I am just having a baby, I can do two things at once very well, thank you!" She walks over to him and gives him a small punch to his jaw. Everyone laughs.

Eddie and Carolyn have quietly listened in on the conversation. Eddie has his arms around her waist as they both face the Masters clan talking and laughing. He leans in to whisper, "Nothing like a big family when there is trouble. See where your adopting Anna has led? Your family has increased ten-fold." He kisses her cheek, from behind.

"Who knew?" is all Carolyn can add. She looks around at all her 'new' family. She would not have met her husband if she wasn't trying to help Anna. Her brother would not have met his wife if not for Anna finding the key to the trunk in the attic which led to asking all the Colonel's siblings to come to his birthday party. She would not have rediscovered her namesake if not for that either. Even if they had reconnected with their EL Dorado family on their own, no one would be

127

helping her brother out of the jam that he is in now, if it weren't for Anna's family. Carolyn leans her head back onto Eddie's shoulder and sighs. "We are a lucky family, no doubt!"

Joshua had come up as Carolyn was saying this. He looked at all the people in the bungalow. "I couldn't agree with you more, sis. We are very lucky, indeed." He calls Helen to him and turns her to them and puts his arms around her waist to mimic his sister and her husband's pose. "I told you, Helen. 'Luckiest man alive'!" He nods to the Masters problem solving HIS problem. He says to them. "I cannot thank you all enough. I almost feel funny going back to Lawrence while you all are working toward proving my innocence. After service tomorrow, I need to go back home to update our books so that our attorney can use them for my defense. We won't be but a few days." He looks to his wife and sister. "Want to go to Lawrence for a few days?"

Helen looks back at him and answers first, "I never want to spend another day or night without you."

Joshua looks at Carolyn, "Well, sis? Don't you have inventions that need to be worked on? OR journals and more letters to bring back to read?" He smiles, "We have to know when and how the Colonel gets his Julia back."

She looks to Eddie. "I'd like to go back for just a night or two, at most. You should stay with the investigation. I will go with Joshua, then load up on reading material and come back in my car. Is that okay with you?"

Matthew steps in, "if it is only a night or two, we can spare our investigative leader. I never want to see couples separated. Byron's men have everything taken care of and you are only a phone call and a few hours away. Go with your wife, please."

Eddie just nods as Joshua repeats, "Luckiest man alive!" as he hugs his Helen, tighter.

TWENTY-SEVEN

An Excerpt from Elizabeth Lewis's Journal
Thursday, November 11, 1880 in Lawrence, Kansas

Will wrote that the five-hundred-mile trip went smoothly. He had enough wagons and horses and Cavalry accompanying him to ensure it. He wouldn't tell me of any major problems, either way. He is very concerned over my sleepless nights.

He arrived at Fort Keogh in just a little over a month's time. That is amazing to move that big of an outfit. He must be a very organized leader. He did not stay in Montana long. Nokomis's husband Kanuna had not traveled that far yet. Little Wolf on the other hand, had.

Little Wolf's four braves surrendered to Will, peaceably. The pact was completed. Little Wolf heard many good things about Navooaleve.

This is Will's name in Cheyenne. It means something like 'too tall'. Will is the tallest of the boys, at six feet six inches. Ian was just a little shorter at six feet three inches. Oh, my Ian! What I wouldn't give to see him again. Joseph took after my side of the family and is only about six feet. Chilly at only thirteen was nearly six feet already so he might get taller than Will. He admires Will so much! He says that he will go into the Cavalry, when he is old enough. What will I do with two of them out there, worry twice as much?

Will said that he will go back to the Pine River Agency to check for Kanuna and Joshua Nathaniel and pick up the other tribesman that will be tried. This trip should be much faster. They will take just one wagon back but have a regiment of men to guard them. Then he will come back to Kansas! We were all very excited at the notion of Will coming home. Especially his Julia.

An Excerpt from a Letter by Julia Johnson

April 21, 1879

My Darling Will,

I must be very cross with you. You did not tell me where to send this letter! I did not know if Fort Keogh was a manned fort but I took the chance that this letter would be waiting for you, when you arrived.

I cannot stay cross with you, my dearest cousin, for very long. Your last letter that told the CORRECT sequence of kisses allowed me to be so . . . warm! And we are having an unusually warm spring here in Lawrence.

I think that Carolyn and my brother are getting more and more serious. He has come out here to visit her twice this spring. He only stays a day or two but they are inseparable the whole time. I know that she is so much younger but she has become so grown up because of his influence. You might scarcely recognize your own little sister except for that red hair! Her hair, it seems, is one of the things that Grant admires the most. Daily, he would comment to me that he has never seen such lovely locks as hers. I am at a complete loss of what to say! He never seemed interested in anyone else's hair, before.

Mother Beth allowed me to see your last letter to her and I am very happy and anxious that our separation will shortly be over. I have been waiting for you for so long my Will.

When we moved to EL Dorado, I was eighteen and of legal age to be wed, as were you. When you did not ask me to stay and be yours, I was devastated. Then I wrote you three long letters, a month apart and I heard nothing from you. Again, the agony of losing you was almost too much to bear. I know that you have already apologized and explained yourself before I asked you to do so and I have forgiven you but . . . I bring this up because I am still waiting.

I know that you said that if I will have you, that we will live happily ever after. I will ask this now so that you can make your decision on the road and not have to face me if the decision goes against me. I ask that if I am to be yours forever that I will not be waiting for you to complete the next campaign during our marriage. I have waited for you long enough and I would like my husband to be at my side for all the big and little things in life; like I have witnessed your father and mother doing, daily.

What I am asking is very large, I know. I am asking you to choose me over the Cavalry. This is the career that you have chosen and I will pack up for El Dorado, if you want to continue your career. I will not fault you. I will not hate you. I will envy the work you love more than you love me.

I need you to make this choice before I see you. I know I am not strong enough to see you and not have you after all the promises and special moments that our lives have shared. I have loved you for so very long, my dearest cousin Will, that I can scarcely breathe knowing that I am risking it all, with this request. I love you and want to live happily ever after WITH YOU BY MY SIDE, not in a campaign that takes you from me for a while or forever. I want you to live and hold me and kiss me and make babies with me and watch them grow as our love grows deeper with every passing year. Can the Cavalry promise you that?

I know that you will be bringing the Cheyenne back to Kansas for their trial. I know that this will be another dangerous mission. Please stay safe, my love. If I never see you again, please have a long and happy life and always stay safe. I will be anxiously waiting for your decision.

Just one more memory before I go. That New Year's Day after our 1st kiss together under the mistletoe, remember? We went on a sleigh ride and you brought hot chocolate and we held hands and looked up at the stars. We kissed several times on that ride. You looked in my eyes and told me for the first time that you loved me. I cried and said it back. You wiped my tears away and told me that you never wanted to make me cry again. I said that they were happy tears but you told me that any tears coming from my eyes splits your heart in two.

Oh, my Will, let it not be true. I am crying now for MY heart is in two from making you make this terrible choice. I am telling you that if you choose me that I will not let you regret *that decision. I will love you all my life and beyond, if possible. I will never let you <u>feel</u> alone, IF you never let me <u>live</u> alone. Please say you will be mine and only mine. Say that we will live happily ever after.*

And I will be all yours,
Julia

An Excerpt from the Telegram from

Major William Lewis

April 25, 1879

My Darling, Darling Cousin Julia,

Please do not cry! (stop)

Please do not pack up for El Dorado!(stop)

I have wired my resignation to General Crook to be effective upon the delivery of the Cheyenne for trial at Dodge City.(stop)

Marry me, immediately upon my return and

We Will Live Happily Ever After!(stop)

Your Will (forever)

TWENTY-EIGHT

November 12, 1939
Sunday in Lawrence, Kansas

After Sunday service, the Lewis couple, the James couple and the Harrick's family all follow each other back to Lawrence, in their separate vehicles. They arrive at about two in the afternoon. They all hurry into the house and Anna goes straight into the kitchen to put Clara Beth on the potty. She is so pleased that the training has been going so well. Henry is in the kitchen with her and goes straight to the pot to make some coffee. He was just thinking that the Colonel and Helen would always have a cup of tea together while the rest of the household drank coffee. He calls out to Helen. "Do you want a cup of tea, Helen? I'll put the kettle on for you."

"Henry, that would be lovely. I will be in the kitchen in a minute." She was in the parlor, staring at the couch that she was sitting on when she learned of her father's death. She can almost feel that sick to her stomach feeling that the news gave her. She puts her hand over her still flat stomach and looks down at her invisible little one and says, "Or was that your sorrow that I was feeling?" She gives her tummy a little pat. "I will make sure that you know all about the bravest man in the world, your grandfather.

"So we are already having regular conversations with our child, are we?" She turns and Joshua is standing behind her with one eyebrow up.

"I have been talking to him or her since the day I found out. I wish I had told you right then instead of running away. I was so foolish." She goes to him, and he takes her in his arms.

"Enough about that, you need not ever mention it again. You are here in my arms where you belong and nothing else matters." He tilts her head up so that he can give her a little kiss. She responds with her arms around his neck and they are momentarily lost in each other. Then they hear the tea kettle whistling from the kitchen.

"Saved by the whistle, my husband. I need a cup of tea, desperately." She wiggles out of his arms like the impatient Clara Beth would and walks determined into the kitchen. "Anna, do you have a cookie to go with that tea? I am in the mood for a little afternoon sweet."

Joshua is tempted to follow her but he must go into the home office. Henry had promised to bring all the ledgers home from the farm office so that Joshua can look them over and tidy things up for the attorney. He is in there for about ten minutes when Helen looks in on him with a cup in her hand. She is smelling it. He says to her, "is your tea to your satisfaction, Mrs. Lewis?"

She smiles, "Yes, it was, but this is a cup of coffee that I brought for you, Mr. Lewis." She put it down and goes to stand behind him so that she can look over his shoulder at the ledgers. "Teach me how you do your accounts. I will need to take over the books in EL Dorado and I need to know how. Do you mind?"

He turns to her and backs up a little, then he pats his lap. "Have a seat and I will gladly show you something." He smiles.

"Joshua, I am being serious, are you? I know that look. We wouldn't be looking at ledgers with that look on your face, will we?" He doesn't answer but stands up and goes to the door and closes it. "Joshua, what are you thinking, it is the middle of the afternoon and you have work to do!" She scolds him.

"I do have work to do, so we'd better not waste any time. Come over here." He reaches for her and she gladly goes to him and she kisses him passionately, but then breaks away.

"I am serious about learning and helping out. I want to be your partner in everything. I want to be a part of this business and the farm business back home. I know Judd and Matthew have been doing it all, all this time, but I want to be involved. Help me with that, please?"

"Of course, Helen. Just so that you know, I can take care of these things for you and you do not have to be burdened with them."

Suddenly, Helen looks as if she is mad. "Joshua, I don't

want you to take care of things for me. I want to be your partner. I *need* to be your partner. I am not a visitor or a china doll or a child. I am your wife and I need more than just waiting for you to come home and *tell* me about the business. I need to participate. Darling, this is one of the things that I was upset about before I left." She admitted it and is worried that he will get mad at her for asserting herself.

"Helen, I love you and I will help you learn, but wait, what? This was '*one of the things*'? What were the others? Please be honest and tell me everything. I don't want you to become unhappy again." He walks over to the desk and moves the chair out for her to sit. He takes his coffee and has a sip, then sits on the edge of the desk while he patiently waits for her to take a seat and explain.

"I feel foolish about it now, Joshua. I felt that I wasn't your partner, I was just a . . . I don't know, I guess a new plaything not a real wife." She blushes at her own bold use of words. He goes to say something but she holds her hand up to silence him. "I also, did not understand the unusual relationship that you shared with Carolyn. I get it now. There *is* nothing better than family. There is one more thing, Joshua and this isn't easy for me to admit. I wasn't jealous of <u>just</u> Carolyn. I knew you loved me but I saw . . . I thought I saw . . . something between you and Anna. She and Henry are so much in love but there was still something I could not put my finger on between the two of you and it was eating me up. So, I will ask you now and be honest. Did you and Anna have a relationship while she was Rosanne?" She let out the breath she was holding but looked down at her lap. She felt ashamed, afraid and foolish all at the same time. A tear found its way to her eye.

"You are smarter than I ever gave you credit for my darling Helen. When Anna first came here, I was confused about my feelings for her. She never was. She knew Henry was out there, somehow, and she knew that her love for him was something all consuming, but what she felt for me was that of a big brother. I didn't believe it or understand it, *at the time!* I do love her, Helen but it is no different than my love for

Carolyn. She is my little sister that was brought back to us." He kneels at her side. "The love that I feel for you, takes my breath away. My heart smiles and beats differently when you are in the room. You are the first thing I think about in the morning and the last thing that I think about before I go to sleep. You are my everything! You have been taking my breath away since you took off that mask at the Colonel's birthday party and it happened again when you brought the coffee cup in the office. I do not know how else to say it. You are the love of my life. I have never felt anything like this and I think that many people go their whole lives without finding it. Anna feels the same way – for her Henry. She and I are siblings, nothing more." He stands up and takes her with him. "Now, Mrs. Lewis, take my breath away and smile for me. Then kiss me so that I know you believe me."

She gladly does so. "I do believe you, Mr. Lewis." She kisses him again, but this time with a great slow tenderness. When she finally pulls away, she smiles and says. "I do believe."

TWENTY-NINE

An Excerpt from Elizabeth Lewis's Journal
Friday, November 12, 1880 in Lawrence, Kansas

Our Major Will has sent a telegram to Julia, asking her to marry him as soon as he arrives home. This was very exciting news but I could not seem to feel happy. I have loved Julia as a daughter her whole life and she is the perfect match for Will. She has been his 'only one' since he met her at seven years old. When her brother, Grant, turned twenty-one, he inherited the family estate in El Dorado. He took his mother, Mary, and eighteen-year-old Julia with him. I thought that it would kill Will to be apart from her. The weeks turned into months then he joined the Cavalry, I think to get her off his mind. He asked her to come stay with me after he went off to hunt the Cheyenne and they started writing each other as often as his movements would permit.

She had been a pleasure to have in my household, helping with the teenagers, the farm and just being a sweetheart about everything. Now, she will be Will's wife. Why did I not feel the happiness for them that I should?

It was the grayness that took hold of me when Ian and Lydia were killed! The news of Joshua Nathaniel's life being spared did not erase the gray. Seeing Carolyn, growing up with her beau Grant at her side did not fight this gray away. Now the news of the marriage did not absolve me of it.

I was thinking that Ian and Lydia would have been so happy to see all these events if only they were still alive. Will I ever get past putting my loss of them in front of all the living going on around me?

There was little time to think about that. It was spring and we had our hands full with the planting and maintaining the ever-growing farm.

My William suggested that we travel to Dodge City to meet Will and attend the trial of our Ian's killers. He wanted to bring Julia to Will, so they could be wed there. I could not think of mixing such sorrow and joy together so far from home. I could not conceive of facing the Indians that were responsible for all those deaths, even though I understood their desperation. How could I couple that with seeing my son Will for the first time in forever and then watch him wed. No, I could not do it. I would not hear of it.

Poor Julia, she was so crushed that I refused to go to Dodge City. She wanted me at her side when she saw Will. She was nervous about his homecoming and this was a way to shorten her wait. She had not seen him in person, since she left Lawrence in 1875! Four years is a lifetime at this age! I had not seen him since January and I could barely hold it in!

But when I refused to go, so did she. She could have gone home to get her mother then go Dodge City. She could have gone with my William and taken Carolyn with her, but she refused all options that did not include me.

How can I crush her so? How could I let my gray, descend upon her happiness, also? How could I face it all? I couldn't. That was all there was to it! The gray won.

CHERISSE M HAVLICEK

An excerpt from the Letters of
Julia Johnson

May 15, 1879

My Darling Will,

My heart was never so glad as to receive your telegram. My hands were shaking so hard that I was scarcely able to open it for fear that it meant that I would never see you again.

When I removed it from its envelope I was disheartened by it being so short. So, little wording could only mean a no!

Oh, with my tearful eyes your words were read.
Oh, to my heart did they speak!
To my lips a smile did spread
and to my knees did they make weak!

My darling Will, I will marry you the first moment we can arrange it! I will be yours forever. I will never leave you since you have promised to do the same. But, I am worried now that since I have given you this ultimatum, you will regret your choice and begin to resent me for making you give up a career that you love. What have I done to you, my Darling? Though I cannot begin to live with you being outside of my reach, I cannot live with thought of you growing to hate me! I feel terrible but wonderful at the same time. I am to be your wife!! How happy you have made me!

Your father was so excited at the news that he offered to take me to Dodge City for us to wed and then he would attend the trial. I thought that it was a splendid idea but for your mother.

I am worried for her Will. She said that she was very happy for us but ran crying from the room at the mention of going to Dodge City. I know that she doesn't want to go to the trial and I understand that but I think it was more than that. Your father was so sweet and he held her as she cried for fifteen minutes. I felt so guilty. How could our happiness cause her such pain? She has always said that she loves me like her own

140

daughter but now that I will be her daughter, officially, it caused her dread.

I told her that we would wait and have the ceremony here in Lawrence when enough time has allowed my mother and brother to attend. I told her that I wanted to wed in the church that she was wed and she put her hand up to her face and cried out. "That's where Ian and Lydia wed!" and ran from the room once again.

That act brought me to a realization. Your mother knows that Ian is gone and a part of her fears being happy because that will mean that his death had no impact on her. In her day to day life, she trudges along but these crucial moments crush her like a heavy stone falling from a high place right upon her. We do not know how to help her when she gets like this.

Your father said that he will still go to Dodge City so he can escort you home. As much as it will tear me up inside, I will wait for you in Lawrence and we must wait to wed. I would not cause your mother another moment of pain, for anything.

I have written my mother and she is preparing to come to Lawrence to stay with Grandmother Marilyn to attend our Nuptials, whenever they take place.

Your short note, though full of promise, told no tale of a memory. Shall I depart one more on you before I leave you (on paper)?

It was the Valentines Dance after our first 'I love you' to each other. I was all dressed to go to the event but I was very ill, when you came to escort me. I had been coughing violently most of the day and had little strength or voice left. It was another February snow storm outside and you refused to let me leave my mother's house. As I tried to voice my objections, you laughed at me for all I was doing was squeaking. I was so mad that you were laughing! I tried to talk over your laughter but that started a coughing fit.

You stopped laughing, walked over to the table and poured water into a cup and made me drink. After I did so, you bent to kiss my forehead. When you felt the heat of my fever, you yelled for my mother and told her that I must be put to bed, *immediately. Then you effortlessly picked me up with loving arms and carried me to my sick bed. You instructed my mother to undress me and put me under warm blankets but that YOU were going to spend the evening at my bedside. Then you added, "PROPRIETIES BE DAMNED! I WILL NOT TAKE NO FOR AN ANSWER!" I think my mother fell in love with you at that moment.*

There you were, an attractive young man, missing a Valentine Dance (with all the pretty young ladies attending), and refusing to leave a sick girl's bedside! As ill as I was, that is one of my fondest memories of you. You are such a caring man. Big heart, as your mother would say.

Please bring that Big Heart home to me. I want you to take me in your loving arms and lay me down and take care of me. I will not object to your staying at my bedside. If I might be so bold, PROPRIETIES BE DAMNED! I WILL NOT TAKE NO FOR AN ANSWER!

Yours forever,
Julia

An Excerpt for the Letters of
Major William Lewis

May 20, 1879

My Sweetest Julia,

Your letter was so full of news and information that I have had to read it and reread it. Thankfully, I have no Privates attending me.

My darling, fear not, you did not force me to make a choice that I will regret later. I have been considering a farmer's life after all this traveling that I have been forced to do, in conditions I would not send a dog out in. I have been dreaming of picking tomatoes, green beans, sunflowers and pumpkins and raising cattle in the Kansas sun.

That is when I am not dreaming of YOU!! I have given enough of my life to the Cavalry and if it wasn't for Joshua Nathaniel, I would have quit and been home last March. The decision was made before you told me that your dream was to have me at your side for once and for all. It's my dream, too.

I have a confession to make. I do regret not finding Joshua Nathaniel. I had such high hopes that he would be at one of the other Indian agencies. I have no leads to follow so I feel I am ending my career without having done the one thing that might make the family happy again. Bringing the boy home to his grandmother! I am almost ashamed to face her. I am so disappointed in myself. I am sure that you, my love, will help me through it all.

I do not know what to do about my mother either. She has suffered so many horrible losses in her life starting with the Quantrill Massacre. I think that they have finally caught up with her. I know that my safety is her big worry and I hope to never have her worry on my account again.

If all goes well, tell my father that I expect to be in Dodge City around the middle of June, give or take. I will wire him when I am about week out so that he can meet me. Tell him to bring Chilly with him. Chilly writes of wanting adventure, he should have a taste of it under Father's watchful eye and I could give them all the details of my travels that are not fit for a woman's ears.

All of me wants to beg you to accompany them, but for my mother's sake, stay at her side. I am so proud of you to not want to hurt her by coming to Dodge City to marry. We will be together for the rest of our lives, my love. A week or month will not a difference, make.

Now for your other suggestions!! You _are_ getting bolder and bolder! I do remember your Valentine illness and I remember you were trying to be brave and go out into the cold so that you could dance with me. It meant so much to you.

I owe you that dance! I owe you many dances for all the Balls we could have attended if not for my stubbornness and my career! I promise to dance with you as often as there is music playing and for a few times when there isn't. I will hold you close and smell your Rosewater perfume, but I will be the one to sneak kisses to your cheek. I owe you that and more

I can hardly believe that we will be together in a month's time. Together and for the rest of our lives, I do solemnly swear, but with one exception, I beg of you. If any news comes regarding my nephew, please allow me to try to find him in an unofficial capacity. I will not answer to anyone but my heart. And IT only answers to you. But, I fear, it will always weigh heavily upon me if I cannot bring the child back to us.

I will close with a memory of the last Valentine Dance before Grant's inheritance and your moving away. You wore a pale blue satin gown with a bodice that showed off your womanly charms. You wore a cameo around your tender neck on a blue silk ribbon, you smelled of Roses and had on blue slippers with a small bow on your tiny feet. Your long locks were once again, piled up upon your head in beautiful rolls that had the same color blue ribbon delicately woven in and out of your beautiful dark shiny hair and you put baby's breath throughout.

As you have always given me a hard time about being eleven months younger than you, that night I felt _years_ younger. You were a grown woman that I had no right to even approach; for you were the most beautiful woman in the room!

How you chose me when you had all of Lawrence at those tiny blue shoed little feet!

As was the dance's custom, I could not be your sole partner for the evening but you did manage to let me dance half of the dances with you. As I was with other partners on the ballroom floor I would get dizzy trying to keep my eye on your every move. To be honest, I was keeping an eye on your dancing partners so that they did not try to take liberties with you. It was a heart wrenching thing watching you in the arms of another!

Thinking of that, I am at a loss at how I let you move to El Dorado and NOT ask you to stay or fight for your affection. I am at a loss at how I lived a single moment without you in my life! How was I so stupid, to have risked your finding love in the arms of someone else?

I have no explanation. I was a complete fool! How you could forgive me or still love me is beyond my understanding! So, I must ask you to look in your heart. Does a part of you hate me for abandoning you? I would never blame you if you did.

I am a stupid, stupid man, in love with a beautiful woman, who captured my heart at seven years old and though I tried to abandon you, that grip on my heart held on.

The memories of you have kept me going in the worst of hard times. Hoping that we could make more memories has given me a will to live, carry on, and make you proud. I owe you everything, even if you decide that I am that lowly deplorable idiot that doesn't deserve to be your doormat.

I have so much to make up for, and so little to offer you. I cannot give you my heart because you have had it for the thirteen of the almost twenty years that it has beat in my chest.

I can only promise to make sure that every day, you will have no doubt of my total devotion to you. You are my everything, my past and my future and the very air that I breathe. I am truly nothing without you. So, I beg of you to be mine, always.

Tell my mother that I love her, and kiss her on the cheek for me. Tell Marjorie and Carolyn I said hello to them, too.
Yours to do with as you will, forever!
Your Will

THIRTY

November 15th, 1939
Wednesday in Lawrence, Kansas

The last few days were very busy. The Legacy Plantation business books were attended to with the help of Henry, Helen and Carolyn. They were ready for the strictest of audits and Helen felt overwhelmed at first but as they went along, she got more and more comfortable with the process. She was so glad at the end of it all that she saw that this farm was a very profitable business. When Miles Curtis came to the farm, Joshua insisted that she explain the Farm's financial status. She was nervous at first but as she started talking about the now familiar accounts and numbers, she spoke with more and more confidence.

Eddie and Carolyn left yesterday afternoon, almost immediately following Mr. Miles' visit. Eddie did not want to be away from the surveillance of the house or their suspect Albert Croner. The Brewster Security Agency had watched him from a hidden place on the 'headache house' property and used their radios to exchange cars when they were following him, so he wouldn't suspect anything. He was eating out and drinking at bars but not doing anything wrong or acting suspicious, yet.

Carolyn had stocked up on letters from the Colonel and his Julia. She needed the next journal of Gram Beth's, also. She only had a few pages left to read in the one that was in EL Dorado. She had brought back the letters that were read and put them away. Anna said that she and Henry will read them when the journal is reunited with them so that they can be read in the order that they so carefully put them in.

There is a cold front that has blown in from the north and the windows of the large plantation home were rattling with the wind. Helen decided to take a walk around the house in the brisk afternoon. Joshua was with Henry looking at some fences that needed repair on the cattle land. They would be back in time for dinner. A little before four, Anna had just taken out the pie and started the prep work for dinner which will be at six sharp. On Sunday night, during dinner, Helen had asked the family if they had any objections to carrying on her father's tradition of a set time for the evening meal. All those present, welcomed it.

Anna was chopping the vegetables, when the kitchen door blew open and Helen tripped over the threshold and fell against the door before hitting the ground. Anna rushed to her side. "Helen, my dear, are you okay?" She helped the young lady up. "What a stumble! Did you hurt yourself? Please, let me get you a chair." She goes to the pantry for a chair, as the stools in the kitchen are all tall for counter sitting. Once Helen was on the chair, Anna pours her hot water for a cup of tea. "What a fall! My goodness. Helen, you are shivering. Here, hold the hot cup while it steeps." She puts the cup in her shaking hands. "Is it that cold out?"

"No, it's just that the fall scared me. All that I could think about is the baby. What if I hurt the baby?"

"Babies are in a pretty solid place and you are still not showing. Your belly did not take a blow. Are you in any pain?"

"No, I just cannot stop shaking. Anna, can I ask you something, personal?"

Anna is back at the chopping board and her back is to her. She turns to her. "I don't see why not, we are family. Go ahead."

"Well, first I want to apologize for my . . . um, mood before I went to EL Dorado. I was a bit of a snit to you. I'd like to explain myself if I may."

"Helen, you don't owe me an apology. We are good. I grew up with Melinda and she would be a bit of a snit, every so often." She walks over to her and gives her a hug. "Don't fret over past. Dream of the future."

Helen smiles. "Dream of the future . . . I like that. I still want to explain but it's embarrassing. Can we go sit on the couch in the sitting room?   Can you leave the food for a minute?"

"Yes, I am ahead of schedule but I do want to put the beef on shortly. We are having roast, tonight, with apple cinnamon pie for desert." She gives the younger girl a little wink. Then she puts her arm in Helen's and gets her off the chair. Anna swoops down to pick up little Clara Beth, and says. "Clara, do you want to play in the sitting room?" Cup in hand, Helen follows Anna with Clara in her arms, to the sitting room. There is a fire started to get the chill out of the room. Anna puts Clara down on the Colonel's old chair to play with her baby dolls. They take their places on the couch.

Helen says, "I am ashamed of my actions. I was under the assumption that . . . um, I wasn't very important to Joshua and I had no part in the running of the household. I felt that he conferred with his sister too much. I was also upset with you. You had such an easy way with him, while I struggled." She looks down at the cup in her hands. She takes a long sip.

Anna blushes. "I am sorry that I upset you. I never meant to do that." She reaches out to hold her hand. "It isn't easy coming into a full household and trying to find your place in it. We have been together for quite a while here but Henry had the same problem, well in reverse. We had our own place when he started to work for Carolyn but then when Joshua took over, Henry had a little issue working with him because of my affection for Joshua when I was Rosanne. It all worked itself out but Henry was very sensitive about it."

"So, I am not the only one that thought that there was something between you and Joshua? Henry thought so also?"

"Oh, Helen.   There was never anything between Joshua and I. Even when I did not know my name or his, I knew that I belonged to Henry. I knew that I had a great love out there somewhere. I could almost picture him. I could hear his voice in my dreams. I was lovesick from missing him, yet I did not know who he was. I was a lost creature in need of protecting and Joshua naturally stepped in to help me. He would help anyone hurt. Henry understands now and . . . now he has another brother besides Matthew. You do not have to worry.

Joshua is yours and yours alone."

"I know that, now. I explained my feelings to Joshua when we got back together but I wanted to clear the air between you and I. I needed to say that I am sorry, to you and say that your PIE smells unbelievable. You are so sweet to make it with cinnamon every time, just because you know that is how I like it. Thank you, Sister." She reaches over to hug the taller slightly older woman.

This catches Anna, a little off guard. "Really, Helen, it's all right. I wasn't upset with you to begin with, and I like to make food that are favorites for people. It is what I do. Now, I need to get back to doing it." She stands up to go and turns to Helen. "Thank you for explaining, and understanding the past as it was. I think you are changing with that baby inside. We kind of 'have' to, don't we? Do you want another cup of tea? I'll put the kettle back on, if you like."

"No, I think this cup is trying to say goodbye, now. I need to go to the bathroom so often, now. Is that normal?"

"Yes, it will get better for a few months, then worse at the end. You have a long road, ahead. I wish I could have another little one. Dr. Mason said that I might not survive another birth. My condition after my rape and coma left me too weak to carry our first child and I was scarred from it. I barely survived Clara's birth. So, Henry begged me not to chance having another one, but it is hard when you love someone so much, it is hard to always be 'careful'. It takes all the spontaneity out of our closeness. Do you know what I mean?" Helen just nods. "I do long for a baby, so yours will be very welcomed here." Anna now surprises Helen with an impromptu hug. "So, after you go potty, more tea?"

Clara Beth wiggles off the chair, "I go potty, Mama, peas?" Anna takes her hand.

"Good thing we have several indoor bathrooms. I will take Clara to the one in the kitchen." She heads off to the kitchen swiftly, still holding Clara's hand. Anna knows that there is little time to waste when Clara makes her announcement.

Once all the women are done and back together in the kitchen, Anna seasons her meat and puts it in the oven to

roast. Helen has that second cup of tea and the girls talk like '
long lost friends, for the first time that they have been living
together.

"Anna, can you teach me to cook? Mattie would not allow
me in her kitchen, and I always wanted to know how."

"Well, the best way to learn is to DO. Let's finish cutting
the vegetables for roasting. I have the potatoes in the oven, but
these do not take as long so they will go in, in a half an hour.
Nothing worse than soggy veggies! Here. Hold the knife, like
this." Anna goes behind the smaller woman and puts her arms
around her to lead her to the correct posture for slicing.

After everything is sliced and put in the oven, Helen says,
"Wait until Joshua finds out that I helped cook! Wait, can we
keep it a secret, until I can make a meal by myself? I can just
see a candlelight dinner for two that I made all by myself. I am
so excited. I will not be able to keep it quiet. Too bad we are
going back to EL Dorado, in the morning.   I want more
lessons."

THIRTY-ONE

An excerpt from Elizabeth Lewis's Journal Monday, November 15th, 1880 in Lawrence, Kansas

My husband William and my youngest son, Chilly, set off to Dodge City upon receipt of Will's Telegram. They arrived a week before the trial began and came into town just the day after Will arrived with the tribesmen that were to stand trial for killing the settlers.

I do wish that I had the strength to have gone with them for I longed so to SEE my boy safe and sound in front of me. William did send a telegram when he had his namesake in sight and it lightened my load.

Julia has been a dear. Though I know that it hurt, she stayed with me instead of meeting Will. I know that it broke a part of her heart and I tried to insist that she accompany the men but she, through her tears of disappointment refused to leave me. She said it would be both of us or neither of us. How I let her down, the poor thing.

With all my menfolk now gone, (Ian dead, Joseph in Wichita, Will, William and Chilly in Dodge City.) I was in charge, of all the day to day activities on the farm. Truly, I do not think that both William and I could have been gone together and still had a farm to come home to; being it was summer time and so much hoeing, the harvesting strawberries and tilling to supervise!

The trial convened on June 24, 1879 with the Honorable Samuel Peters of the 9th Kansas District Court presiding. Immediately, defense attorney J.G. Mohler (appointed counsel) petitioned for a change in venue on the grounds, that Judge Peters had 'social contact' with the aggrieved parties. Mohler further claimed that the tribesmen could not get a fair and impartial trial in the two other Districts in Western Kansas so to my HORROR, they were granted a change of venue to the 4th Judicial District of Douglas County!

For all my fear and refusal to be near or close to the

proceedings, the Proceedings were moved HERE! When we got the telegram from William explaining this, Julia laughed and made the comment that 'God moved the mountain to Mohammed!' I admit it, I did see the comparison!

So, William, Will and Chilly were on their way home. Will was officially out of the Army with the transport of Wild Hog, and the braves to Dodge City. They did not tally for they knew that I was missing Will and that Will was missing his Julia.

An Excerpt for the Letters of
Julia Johnson

June 25, 1879

My Dearest Will,

I am so relieved that your official duties are over and you are free to come back to me. Please, do so safely but swiftly. I cannot imagine going another day without you in it. My heart longs for you so.

The change of venue is very hard on Mother Beth and I have tried not to be overjoyed at your homecoming in front of her but overjoyed is an understatement. I am unable to breathe for that first look of you after so many years apart.

My mother is here and we will be united, in marriage as we have been united in heart, as soon as we can arrange it. Mother and Gram Marilyn have been sewing a proper wedding dress for me. It is so beautiful and I wish that I could meet you while wearing it so that I will be as beautiful as possible. I do not want to disappoint you.

I must confess a deep dreaded secret. A part of me is worried that after our years apart, that we have built up this longing between us that is like a balloon waiting to be popped. We have both blown all this air in it until it cannot hold any more and is about to burst. What if it bursts and all we have left is air? What if after you see me for the first time, none of your feelings for me are really there? What if this is something that we have both built up and neither can hold up to the image that we have created in our minds from the desperation of wanting a rekindled childhood romance? My heart is breaking at the thought of it, I want you to love me so!

I want you to give you a way out. If at any time, after we meet that you feel that this is not the love that you imagined or want, you may slip a note under my door and just write on it that you have changed your mind. I will pack up and leave so *that it looks as though it is my doing and you may save face with your family. You are held in such high esteem by them that it would crush me to think that I could cause a slip in that esteem.*

I will not hold you to your promises that were made in our time of longing. I will understand that the Julia of your beloved childhood is only that - a favorite childhood memory. But I pray that it will never be so!

I will plan on leaving for EL Dorado before we are wed. This will give you time to assess your true feelings for me after having met me and getting to know me again. That sounds like the fairest way to do it. I will leave one week after your arrival and if you want me to come back to you, just send for me and I will be on my way to you to stay.

Yours forever
Julia

An Excerpt from the Letters of
Major William Lewis

June 28, 1879

Dearest Julia,

    I have no doubts that my feelings for you will be genuine and not a balloon. Are your feelings for me wavering?

    I am so sure of my feelings for you that I will insist that you do not plan any trip to El Dorado. Plan instead a honeymoon trip. I would like to travel to Wichita and see my brother Joseph and sister Lizzie as I have not seen either of them in years, nor have I met Joseph's new wife Katherine. Do you think that my love for my siblings may have changed through our absence of each other? This is utter nonsense! Love doesn't work that way.

    May I never hear of such nonsense from your lips, again. I have always loved you, I love you today and will love you until my dying breath.

    I cannot wait to show you just how much I love you and I will continue to show you my love every day that I look upon that beautiful face, if you will be so kind as to allow me that honor!

    In case you need a way out, as you put it, I will allow you to put a note under my door and I will be forever grateful to you for saving my miserable life through the memories and letters but I will not hold you to any of the promises given in those letters. But I pray that it will never be so.

    We will be leaving Dodge City, tomorrow, and I hope that the horses will carry us as swift as they can, so . . .

    I will be forever in your arms within a week's time.

Your Will.

THIRTY-TWO

November 16th, 1939
Thursday in EL Dorado, Kansas

Melinda is at the Johnson farmhouse with the ledgers of the farm accounts and is sitting on the couch with a ledger on her lap. Susan is across from her, looking at a second ledger. "I am glad for a pair of fresh eyes. I feel I have looked these over so much that I am not even seeing the numbers anymore."

Matthew walks in with Katie Ann on his hip and sees his sis lounging. "Melinda, the ledger barely fits on your disappearing lap. Is the babe looking over the accounts, also?"

"Yes, see Susan, you have two pairs of fresh eyes. I hope one of us catches a break. We do not have much time. We've lost a week already. Poor Joshua, no one can be farther from a cold-blooded killer than he is."

"I agree. Susan where is Katie Ann's bag? I am smelling a change is needed."

Susan goes to get up but Matthew just puts his hand up. "Stay at the books, I'll change her if you tell me where the bag is at." Melinda gives a chuckle. "What? Don't you think I can change a diaper?"

Melinda laughs. "Matthew, it was decided four years ago, that you can do anything you set your mind to, except give birth to a baby!"

Both Susan and Matthew freeze in place to give Melinda the strangest look.

***

After several days of nothing happening, with the surveillance of Albert Croner, Eddie decided to take a more active part. The Brewster Agency provided him with a 2-way radio, and he used one of their cars to share the rigors of the 24-hour surveillance.

His first time out, Eddie is behind Croner leaving the

'headache house'. Jason, the other detective on duty, and he are to switch out multiple times so that Croner does not suspect a tail. Eddie gets back behind him just as they are approaching the downtown corner of Main and Central. Croner finds a parking spot next to the Citizens State Bank. Eddie also parks but he is across the wide expanse of Main Street. Though the rest of the detectives are told to follow only, Eddie thinks that Croner entering a bank can be significant, so he exits the vehicle and crosses the street. He approaches slowly to look in the bank's windows. Croner is in the center of the lobby at the counter with deposit slips and check request forms.

Eddie enters the building and walks over to the same area as Croner. Eddie takes a pen out of his pocket and asks Croner to hand him a deposit slip. While he is bending to retrieve it from the cubby hole under the table, Eddie leans over to see the numbers and name that Croner was writing on the deposit slip. All he had time to see is that Croner was depositing $2000! Eddie then pats his pockets and says to Croner, "I must have left my wallet in the car." Then he leaves. He waits outside near the window and peeks in to see which teller that Croner will use. Eddie hopes that he will pick one of the young, pretty ones that will be repulsed if he tries to sweet-talk her.

When Croner turns away from the teller, to leave, Eddie hurries to his vehicle and crouches down. He radios Jason to take over the tail from this point. Once Croner's vehicle is out of view, Eddie leaves his car and goes into the coffee shop to use the pay phone. He is only on the line for a few minutes then goes back into the vehicle and radios Jason that he was available, again, to participate in the tail.

***

Matthew hangs up the phone and turns to his sister. "We must leave you to the ledgers, then. Katie, Susan and I are needed elsewhere." With no other explanation than that, they are bundled up and are out the door.

Within 15 minutes, Matthew drives up to the bank with

Susan and Katie Ann. They all walk in and go to the teller that had waited on Croner.

Susan stays a step behind Matthew. Little Katie is trying to go by her father. When she is reaching out for him, Matthew says to the teller, "Excuse me, Miss, I hope you can help me with a very delicate situation. My wife Susan has been harassed by a certain fella and I think that he took some money she was saving up to buy us a house. She has had a small mistrust of Banks since the crash, you know, for the last ten years or so; this is a rough terrible setback." He turns to Susan. "Honey do you want to tell her from here?"

Susan makes a point to give Katie Ann to Matthew then takes a handkerchief from her purse. She pretends to sniffle and dabs her eyes and nose. "I feel like such a fool. I was tending to little Katie Ann, then this brute of an ignorant man comes right into my house . . . <u>our</u> house and he . . . grabbed me and . . ." She looks around to see if anyone else can hear with real tears coming down her cheeks. "He forced himself on me. He then told me that he knew that I didn't trust banks and he knew that I had cash saved up." She sniffles again and wipes her tearing eyes. "He swore that he would hurt Katie and . . . use me again." She turns to Matthew. "I can't go on, please don't make me." She hides her face in her handkerchief.

The teller says quietly. "Have you gone to the authorities? Surely, they can help."

Susan continues to cry into the handkerchief and Matthew puts his hand on her shoulder. He moves forward to talk with the young teller.

"We have gone to them but it is our word against his. We need proof, and I thought that maybe the scumbag deposited our money here? If he has, can you give us some sort of print-out to prove that the funds are here?"

"I don't know if I am allowed." She says as quietly as a mouse. "I'll have to talk with the Bank Manager, Lois."

Matthew continues, "Look, you'd remember this guy. He is a creep! He's had many women cringe as he tries to force himself on them. He was in here not that long ago. His name is Albert Croner."

She winces.

"I see that you are familiar with him." She shudders, now "Yup, you are very familiar. He is a beast, and if you can picture him touching you against your will, you must help me get him locked up. If he can force himself on my wife with my daughter within sight, he doesn't deserve to roam free."

She is nodding.

"Now, when he was here, did he make a deposit or withdrawal?"

"A Deposit."

"Was it for the full $2000 that he took?"

She gasps. "Yes, it was. I am so sorry."

"Can you provide me with a bank statement showing this deposit?"

"I cannot do it today. The account isn't a personal one – it is a business account. I will need to see if he is the only signature owner before I can give you anything. Besides, the funds are not officially available for twenty-four hours. But if you come back to me tomorrow. I will have three months of statements for you. If he did that to her, maybe he's done this to someone else."

Susan looks up from her handkerchief. Her eyes are red and tearing. The onion juice that she put on her handkerchief, worked well. She looks up at the teller. "I am overcome with your kindness, my dear. With your help, we are one step closer to putting him behind bars, where he belongs."

That statement had every ounce of truth in it.

THIRTY-THREE

An Excerpt from Elizabeth Lewis's Journal,
Tuesday, November 16, 1880 in Lawrence, Kansas

The great homecoming was short lived. Will was barely home for two weeks when an Army friend wired that a white man's boy was seen with the Cheyenne back in the Lakota Territory.

Julia had such trepidation of seeing her Will again after all the years apart, but the years melted away as he dismounted from his horse and took her in his arms. He held her at arms-length, looked her over, up and down and shouted, loud enough to be heard in Missouri. "I am the luckiest man alive!", then, he kissed her in front of everyone. I am not surprised in the least that she accepted that kiss, and put her arms around his neck and unashamedly kissed him back. I recall doing the same when my William came back home from War.

The nuptials took place on Saturday, July 12th 1879. Reverend Richard Cordley presided over the ceremony as he did for my wedding, Father Clyde's to Mother Marilyn, as well as Ian's to Lydia. The reception took place at the former City Hotel, which was newly remodeled. It was a hard event for me, for it brought back so many memories of Ian and Lydia. I tried very hard not to let any of it show for the bride and groom's sake, but I felt like I was dying from it all.

William, of course, knows my plight. He knows that I over-feel much of late. He held me up in church and stayed at my side at the reception and held me in his arms the whole night, afterward. Such a sweet loving man! Julia has one just like him.

The next day, Will and Julia went to Topeka for a few nights, they came home to get ready to go to Wichita to see

Joseph, his new wife Katherine, and Lizzie. The siblings are both doctors there, in a small office that they started. Lizzie is an obstetrician. I had to look it up when she told me that she wanted to be one. It is a women's doctor. Yup, she delivers babies for a living! Well, she helped deliver several of mine!

The night before they left for Wichita, the telegram came. Will looked at his bride who was crying at the thought of his leaving. She dried her tears and said, "This is the one exception that I promised to allow you. You must leave me, for Joshua's sake." Will looked so relieved that she gave him permission while still technically on their honeymoon. She's braver than I!

I swallowed hard for as much as I want Joshua found, I did not want Will gone! Then he said the most ridiculous thing! He wanted to take Chilly with him!!! He said that Chilly and Willie together will be unbeatable! My husband, as he always does in moments of MY crisis was very happy for the youngster. He told me that Chilly isn't cut out to be a great student like Joseph or Lizzie, he was made for adventure and being a force for justice. I wondered what cowboy novel my William got that notion from?

Three days later, Will and Chilly were off on their Indian Adventure to find Joshua. Chilly is now over six feet, so Will chided him about trying to take his Indian name, Navoualevé, which means 'too tall'. Chilly was not quite thirteen years old, and in so many ways was just like this brother, with whom he shares a birthday.

Julia was not at all happy to see Will leave after having just gotten him back and pronounced hers. But she just kept saying that a promise was a promise, as long as, he swears that he will come back as soon as he can.

I could not see them off, it was too much like seeing Ian, Lydia and Joshua off. I think I knew that something would happen to that trio. I could not shake a feeling of dread after they left. Now I was feeling that again. My William said that it is just me worrying and missing them. I prayed that he is right and I am dead wrong. I don't think that I could survive another loss!

I needed to be brave for Julia. Her mother had returned to EL Dorado after the wedding, and I am her mother in all things now. She, the poor thing, was trying to be brave for me the whole time.

It was an act that she could not keep up for very long. A month of waiting for word from her Will went by before she got very sick on us.

Finally, we received a telegram from Will that he and Chilly were fine, but the band that had the white man's boy in it left that area.

I wanted to send a telegram for him to come home to his wife, but Julia made me promise not to send it. She was so sick and being so brave. Part of me wondered if Will would forgive me if something happened to her while he was gone and I did not tell him of her illness.

But Julia got better, thank God. One morning, she came out of the bedroom looking so much better and said, "See, we would have worried Will for nothing!" What a truly brave young lady she is!

If only Will knew what she was going through, if only any of us knew.

An Excerpt from the Letters of
Major William Lewis

August 18, 1879

Dearest Julia,

Chilly and I are staying a few days here at Fort Robinson to get provisions and to hire a Cheyenne or Lakota scout to aid in our search for Joshua. Chilly has been a great help. He has great respect for Indians and they can sense that about him as they sensed it about me. He made a great friend of one brave, Whistling Wind. He might be the one to accompany us but he is young and I do not think that he will be as much help as a tracker as an older brave would be.

The land is so different than my last time through here. That was in the dead of winter as you may recall but now the air is so wet and heavy that I have trouble breathing it. But do not fear, I am living off the thought of you, to be bothered by it.

I am glad of a chance to write to you again. I feel we are our most honest selves in these letters. At least I am. I get embarrassed to say the things out loud that I think to put into words on paper. I think the same holds for you, too.

Those first few days of seeing you for the first time were magic for me. I was not worried of not loving you upon sight but of your not loving me!

Your tear streaked face that was my last vision of you - haunts me. Your tears still cut to my heart. Even the happy ones at our wedding. But, knowing that I caused those last tears by leaving you makes me feel so guilty! I am so sorry for putting us through this separation, yet again.

Please my dearest, forgive me and write to me here at Fort Robinson, I will check back here as often as I can, if for nothing as to get a post from your sweet hands.

I enjoy your missives so very much that I think that when I return home for good that we should continue to write each other. We should do so each week for the first year, I think. This way when we are old and have lost the newness of our love's first passion that we will be able to bask in it from these letters.

I pray that you are doing well despite my absence. I pray that you will continue to love me and pray for my safe return to you.

Please continue the prayers that I find young Joshua, healthy and well cared for and that I will be able to secure him from his captures and bring him back to the bosom of those that have loved him since before he was born.

I must close this letter but I must tell you some good news. I have heard from General Crook and he said that he has put in a request to promote me to Colonel for my services in the Cheyenne war! I told him that I will not come back to service at any rank but it would be an honorary promotion, only. That means no commitment from me but also no monetary increase either. But, I like the sound of that 'the Colonel' - Mother will be so proud!

And what about you my sweetheart? How have you been faring since our separation? Are you being brave for Mother? I did not want to take her Chilly from her but he was talking about running away and I thought that it would be somewhat safer under my watchful eye.

I suppose it is time to tell you of a warming memory, but this time of year, I'd like it to be a cooling memory. The memory I choose is our wedding day. I hated that you decided to spend your last night as a single girl, staying with your Grandmother and Mother at their small cottage. I hated that you did not come for breakfast and that I had to wait until ten a.m. to see you. I hated that when I did see you walking down the aisle, I could not see your face for the thick veil that was covering you.

My heart leapt as your brother (standing in for your deceased father) gave you 'away' to me. I felt as though I was marrying a stranger for you could have been anyone under that awful veil. But, it wasn't just anyone, it was my ONLY ONE!

When I lifted that veil to kiss you as man and wife, my heart was so happy that I thought it would beat out of my chest. Is anyone as lucky as me? I did not want to leave your side that day. I could not wait until nightfall when I could take you in my arms!

When we were finally by ourselves, you were so shy as I approached you for the first time. I could not believe that you waited for me all those years and remained true to me. Now, I mistreat you still by making you wait, once more.

Now, I am remembering how I took you in my arms. How you surrendered to me so completely. I know that it is improper to talk about these things but I was and am in awe of the gift that your love has given me. I am your slave and forever in your debt.

But I must wait to prove that devotion to you once again. I must wait to hold you in my arms and smell your Rosewater perfume and help you let down your beautiful long hair then release you from your frock. Oh, the memories that you have given me!

I cannot wait until I return to you to stay forever more!

Yours to do with as you will,
Your Will

P.S. Chilly says hi, sis!

An Excerpt from the letters of
Julia Lewis

August 23, 1879

My Darling Husband,

I am so relieved that you are thus far in good health and nature. I have taken to worrying for you so much. Mother Beth must be rubbing off on me. I will write to you as often as possible and this way you will have a stack of letters waiting for you at the Fort.

We are thrilled for you that they are going to make you a Colonel!! I am married to a Colonel. I love the idea and I love that I will not have to worry about you on official Colonel duties, even more!!

I must admit that I have been under the weather as of late. Mother Beth wanted to tell you (so that you'd come home) but I would not let her. You would not forgive me if you had to cut your search short of finding Joshua. I would not do that to you for anything in the world.

But I am not myself. I blame it on not having you by my side. We had so little time together as man and wife. I remember and loved every minute of those days. I could not have asked for a more patient man in life or sharing my bed.

And it is too warm to be reliving these memories. Kansas also has been unusually warm these days and I must say that might be a part of my malaise. I am without ambition or strength. Mother Beth has been taking very good care of me.

There is only one thing that will make me better than ever and that is to have you back in my arms, once again.

Do look high and low for our nephew. Do not leave a stone unturned. Be as vigilant as you can, for I want the young boy found and you back at my side and in my bed.

I do agree that it is easier to commit our feelings on paper when nerves do not inhibit us. I have been so very bold in these letters. I can scarcely believe some of the things that I have admitted to wanting from you.

So, let me be bold, some more. I want you to hold me and touch my face as tenderly as you did on our wedding night. I want you next to me so that I can warm my cold feet and I promise to warm you in return, my wonderful husband.

Until you return I will continue to feel like a fish out of water, floundering upon the shore. Please be safe and come back to me. Come put me back in the glorious water of our love's ocean.

Forever Your loving wife (Oh, what a wonderful title!)
~~Your~~ The Colonel's Julia

THIRTY-FOUR
November 17ᵗʰ, 1939
Friday in EL Dorado, Kansas

Matthew is back at the bank just a little past noon. The teller has the documents for him. She said that her manager, Lois, told her to cooperate with giving all the evidence that they have. Lois had worked the fields with Croner and had to quit because she could not stand his touching her every chance he got. This is her way of getting back.

Croner was the only signer on the account listed as Acron Dry Goods on the statements. Matthew heads directly to Helen's house with it. They need to look for matching deposits against the expense records. Susan and Helen go straight to work on them.

Helen is on the floor with the account ledger and Susan is on the couch in Grant's office. Susan says, "This is an unusual deposit amount. Do you have anything for two hundred and twelve dollars?"

Helen takes a sip of her hot tea before answering. "I have a check written for Acorn – no - Acron Dry Goods for that amount."

Susan says, "You know, that I have seen this name so much in these ledgers but I always assumed it was Acorn. There is an Acorn Dry Goods out of Wichita. I thought that this was that legitimate business. What day was the deposit?"

"That was deposited on September 18ᵗʰ when was the check written?"

"September 15ᵗʰ. I need to look for more Acron Dry Goods checks. Acron is short for 'A Croner' is the obvious owner of a dry goods store, somehow. If it were a real business, wouldn't he have deposits from other people or institutions?"

Eddie just returned from his turn tailing Croner and is standing in the doorway, watching over the ladies working. "If he were a real business, yes. But he is using the business name as a beard, to be paid without a noticeable trace. Look how long it took for us to find it."

Helen says from the floor. "I see bi-monthly payments, always written on the 1st and the 15th. Always for just a couple of hundred dollars, never the amount that he deposited yesterday. Where did he get that much?"

"It was a cash deposit, not a check. I saw that on the deposit slip. Does your father have a petty cash account that he keeps here in the house or in a safe?"

"Papa kept a small amount of cash in a tin in the bottom drawer of his desk." She says as she opens the drawer to find the tin, empty. She holds it upside down. "He always kept a little over a thousand, sometimes two thousand in here." She puts the tin on the desktop. "More cash would be in the main safe . . . I haven't thought about it in years!" She gets up and pulls the cord for Sullivan. She is still standing with her hand on the rope as he swiftly enters the office.

"Mistress?" He asks simply.

"Sullivan, when this room was ransacked that night, was the tin out of the drawer?"

"Yes, Mistress, Iz told the sheriff how much Master Grant kept in it but they wuz more interested in hearing about the angry Mister Joshua."

"How much was in there?" Eddie asks.

"Master Grant had just put twenty-five hundred in it the morning before."

"There you have it; he is living off the five hundred and has deposited the rest. We just need more proof."

"Sullivan, isn't there a safe in Papa's room?"

"Yes, Mistress."

"Do you know the combination?"

"No, mistress. It don't have a combo-nation, it has a key. Master Grant kept it on his pocket-watch fob."

"Do you know where the pocket-watch fob is? I do not recall seeing it with his other jewelry."

"He kept the pocket watch beside his bed at night, but he might still had been wearing it when . . . IT happened." He is shaken by his own words. "I am sorry, Mistress."

Helen turned white and sat down. "The police detective

gave me back his personal affects in a manila envelope. I carried it home from the station, the day we were interrogated. I don't remember seeing it after that. Sullivan, do you know where that envelope could be?"

"Iz took it up to Master Grant's room. Iz didn't open it, mistress. Iz thought that you would since it had hiz wallet and other things that he carried with him in it."

"Like his pocket-watch?" She says with a sob.

"Yes, Mistress." Sullivan sobs too.

Eddie, leans in and puts his hand on the sentimental taller man's shoulder. "You're a good man, Sullivan. I'm sorry, but I need you to show me that envelope and where that safe is, please."

Susan interrupts. "Matthew, you need to get to your afternoon class, don't you?"

"I guess, I do. I will come right back here when I am finished. Try not to solve the mystery without me." He turns to leave. "On second thought, just solve the case!! My brother, Joshua's life depends on it!" He grabs his hat and coat and leaves.

Eddie turns back to the servant. "Sullivan, can you lead the way?

"Yes, of course, Professor, sir." They head up the stairs to the master suite.

"Sullivan, just call me Eddie, please."

"No sir, it wouldn't be right. Iz have respect for my betters."

Eddie stops in his tracks. They are in the hallway outside of Grant's master bedroom. "Sullivan, let's get something straight, here and now - no one in this house is your 'better'. We might be more educated but that doesn't make any of us better. You are a kind and loyal person, whose mission has been the comfort of others, his whole life. I said it earlier, you are a good man, Sullivan, but let me say that unequivocally you are my equal in every way."

Sullivan turns to him. "See sir, youz are better, I do not know what that word 'un-quiver-something' means." He smiles, sheepishly, as he says this.

Eddie laughs. "That just means 'without a doubt' my good man. You are without a doubt, unequivocally, my equal in every way . . . in here." Eddie puts his hand up to Sullivan's heart and pats it. "And that is the only measure of a man that I look for. Now stop dilly-dallying, we need to open that safe and see if there are any clues in it."

Helen took a few moments to compose herself downstairs, before following them. She heard the exchange between the two men from the staircase. *Why did I not realize that they were just like us? Why did I assume that they were just 'our servants' not real people with feelings?"* She feels ashamed the way she has always treated Sullivan and his mother. *I must make it up to them, as soon as Joshua is in the clear."*

She follows them into the bedroom. She has not been in here since Mr. Kirby was over. The suits that they had taken out and laid on the bed were all put back. Everything was as neat as a pin.

She stands in the doorway, almost afraid to enter the room. On the main dresser was the envelope from the police. She didn't even see it when she was in here with the undertaker. Sullivan picks it up and turns to Eddie. She crosses the room and takes the envelope from the men. "Please?" She says simply. She moves to the bed and sits down as she tears open the seal. She spills out its contents onto the bed. His belt, wallet and pocket-watch were there as well as his everyday cufflinks and the matching tie tack. His tie was the last thing to fall out of the envelope. She picks up the tie. It is the blue paisley one that he wore when they had dinner the last time. She sees blood splatter on it and drops it like a hot potato. She looks over at the belt and fob chain and they also have blood splatter on them. "Oh my poor Papa!" She says as she falls on the bed to weep.

Joshua enters the room. "What is going on?" He rushes to his bride's side.

Eddie looks to him, "Sorry Joshua, Helen just opened the envelope that contained the things that her father had on him the night of the . . . That night. We are looking for the key to the safe that is in this room somewhere."

Helen lifts off the bed and holds out the pocket-watch fob. She is still crying but she leaves the bed and crosses to the picture of her mother on the wall across from the bed. She pulls on the right side of the picture and it swings open to reveal a safe. She wipes the tears from her eyes as she fumbles with the watch and the small key attached to it.

Joshua is at her side, immediately. "You know the Colonel had a safe key on his watch fob, also. It belonged to a gun safe, but still." He takes the watch and key from her hands and gives her a reassuring hug. "Let me, darling, please?" She leans in on him and he bends down to kiss her forehead. "It will be okay, Mrs. Lewis. Whatever happens, it will be okay."

She smiles up at him, weakly. "I do believe. Mr. Lewis." She watches as he puts the key into the safe and turns it.

He opens it and stands back for Eddie to see the contents. "Looks like a lot of cash in here. There are a few papers besides." He reaches into the safe and removes the money. Here Helen, hand this to Eddie to count, please." He reaches in again. This looks like that insurance policy that will make you a millionaire, Helen. Here is another paper. Oh, this looks like his Last Will and Testament."

"Why didn't Papa's lawyers tell me of a Will?"

"They were not the ones who wrote it. A firm out of Topeka, wrote it, it seems. They must not be aware of his passing. There is something else, here. It's a small envelope. It has your name on it, Helen." He turns to hand it to her.

Her hand is trembling as she takes it. "I can't, please open it and read it to me, Joshua." She hands it back to him and goes back to the bed and sits on it. She brings her hands to her face, while she braces herself for the words.

Joshua goes to her and sits down next to her and opens the note.

> "Dearest Juliet Helen, there is so much that I should be saying to you, but none of the words are coming to me. I have been suffering for so long and I could not take it any longer. I have cancer in the brain like my two dear departed Aunts. I felt this needed to be done while the Farm is asleep and you are safe, sound and

happy in your husband's arms in Lawrence. Please do not blame me for the steps that I have taken. Destroy this note as soon as you read it and do not look for my killer. I have paid him to take me out of my misery but if the insurance company finds out, they will not pay out. Remember to destroy this note. My girl, I have done all this for your well-being. If you do not undo all that I have put in place, you will be set for life. Not that your husband could not provide for you. I am glad that you are happy and safe in Lawrence and I feel free to leave you in his care. I started this plan a year before you met Joshua. He is a fine young man and will help you with everything you need but I wanted to make sure that you were independently wealthy aside from *his* assets.

Please do not blame me for doing this horrible deed. Do NOT look for my killer. Destroy this note. I am in the arms of your mother, where I have dreamed of being for a very long time and I am no longer suffering those terrible headaches and you are rich beyond compare. All I ask of you is to DESTROY THIS NOTE. And forgive me.

Your loving Papa

Eddie is the first to speak. "Wow, I would have never guessed. We have some decisions to make."

Helen looks at him with tear filled eyes. "NO, I have his killer to find. I KNOW Papa tried to stop his date with death, because of my presence, he would not have done this with me not – how did he put it 'HAPPY AND SAFE IN LAWRENCE'. *But* he was killed, anyway. This note means nothing, other than proving that he was a desperate man that someone took advantage of. Albert Croner, has to be his killer. He took the twenty-five hundred dollars as his pay-off! Sullivan heard Papa say 'Stop for my Juliet Helen's sake!'"

Sullivan who was a silent witness to all this says with disgust in his voice, "I know'd that Croner. He'd been here a few times and I said to Master Grant that he should not be seen with his likes. Poor white trash is all he is! Low down dirty white trash."

They all look at the six-and-a-half-foot black man with their mouths open.

"Truer words have never been spoken, my good man! We just have to prove it, somehow." Says Eddie.

THIRTY-FIVE

An Excerpt from Elizabeth Lewis's Journal
Wednesday November 17, 1880 In Lawrence, Kansas

Our daily lives are so hectic in the late summer. So much to be done on the farm and with the cattle getting larger by the day, that sometimes we can barely manage a meal by the time we fell into bed. Such was our life last August when Julia got so sick that she was not able to hide it any longer.

Her energy level and good cheer dwindled by the day. She had rallied a bit after Will's first telegram but did not stay there for long. I was forbidden to contact Will but I was so anxious over her condition that I contacted my Lizzie.

Upon receipt of my letter, Lizzie telegrammed that I should bring Julia to her, immediately!! I was not prepared for that and neither was Julia. She had written to Will that she was doing so much better and worried that he would find out if she saw Lizzie, professionally.

Even with all the duties of the farm weighing on me, I saw no option but to drop everything and take Julia to El Dorado to retrieve her mother then accompany them both to Wichita.

As proud as I was to see my Doctor daughter Lizzie, I was just as worried for my daughter Julia. After, a thorough examination, Lizzie, insisted that Julia be hospitalized for a brief time for a procedure. Though she never confided in me, she was suffering from her courses being unabated. Poor Julia was beside herself that her 'woman's condition' would leave her barren. Lizzie tried to give her reassurances but you know us Lewis women - we are the definition of Worry!

We stayed in Wichita for three weeks and Lizzie's procedure seemed to clear up Julia's complaints and we headed to El Dorado to drop off Mary. We stayed in El Dorado for two weeks, *as the travel did use up all of Julia's regained strength.*

In the meantime, Will, had telegrammed home that he heard of another sighting of a white man's boy, this time near the Apache territory. Now mine and Julia's worry increased ten-fold. We have not heard of any fair treatment of the white man among the Apache and Will and Chilly were going to attempt to bargain with them!

Of all her worrying and begging everyone to not tell Will, he found out anyway and as I predicted was more than a little disturbed with me that I did not keep him abreast.

When we arrived back home that first week in October, Will and Chilly were impatiently waiting for our return!!

An Excerpt from the letters of
Colonel William Lewis

October 12, 1879

My beloved,

I am leaving Fort Dodge for the Dakota territory, today. As you know, I have had several scouts out looking for Joshua Nathanial while I was away from my mission. I have heard of two different sightings of my young nephew and was not too sure which to follow up until the scout said that the name of the boy was Harkahome! I may have found him at last!!

I wish to spend the rest of this letter, telling you to never ever withhold vital information from me again! I did not chastise you in person, due to your ill health but as is our custom, I am free to be so much bolder in our letters. If I find out that you have lied to me or omitted some important fact of your health or condition, I will take you . . . and . . . and still love you for the rest of my life. Did I scare you even a little?

As far as your condition, I know that you are concerned about our having children. Do not fret in the least about it, my beautiful wife, I am content that you be healthy, and next to me to have you and hold you until death us do part. I want you beyond that, you promised to stay with me longer, if you go before me, if you recall, and I will hold you to it.

You had asked repeatedly, how I heard you were ill and here is the course of events:

Chilly had heard from Carolyn that she was upset that she was not allowed to go to El Dorado with Mother and Julia. I knew that something was amiss. For one thing, at that time of year, Mother would only leave the farm for a DIRE reason, not bringing Carolyn to see her beau confirmed it. I telegrammed

Lizzie of my worry and she admitted that you were treated and released from her care in improved health.

Chilly and I raced home. We could have been Pony Express Riders for our speed a horse could only have been matched by them. When we arrived in Lawrence to find that you were still not there, a panic once again spread through me but was relieved again by Grant's response via telegram. Thank god for telegrams! I knew that you were healthy again and will arrive in the next day or two. I just needed to wait.

Oh, how hard it is to wait!!! But who am I telling? You have waited for me forever, it must seem so unfair that I am putting you through this, yet again!

Now that it is getting colder out here, I will take the time to tell of a warming memory. I was thinking about when we were barely teenagers. There was a summer picnic put on by Reverend Cordley and the Plymouth Congregational church. It was a very warm August, (aren't they all?) and Mother had made her fried chicken and you and your mother were bringing fruit salad with marshmallows, do you recall? You wore a pale, yellow frock with a small white lace on the modest bodice. The dress had a very large bright yellow ribbon that tied into a huge bow in the back. You were the picture of summer loveliness! As usual, you put light little flowers in your hair. After the meal, we wondered into the glen on our own. We picked wild baby's breath and you let me put them into the curls of your long hair piled atop your tiny head.

We were sitting in the glen together. You thanked me for decorating your hair more than it was. I gave you a tiny kiss on the back of your hand. I was going to kiss you on the mouth but just as our lips were going to touch, my little sisters found us and jumped on us and the flowers came out of your hair. You were so upset with their nonsense. I chased them away and redid a few of your curls, the flowers and the baby's breath. I did my best to make it resemble as it was before but then your mother was calling you and you had to hurry off. I was so close to a real kiss from you!

When I get home, I will be able to place that lost kiss upon you. There will be many more kisses to follow my darling, I promise.

Your devoted servant and loving husband
Will.

An Excerpt from Julia Johnson Lewis

October 20, 1879

My Dearest Darling Will,

I just received you letter of the 12th, thank you for explaining the mystery of your knowledge of my ailment. I promise to be as forthcoming as I can be from this point forward.

So, now, I just fibbed. I will not have you deter from your last and final mission until it is completed. I want my nephew found more than anything. He needs to be back in the bosom of his family, for his sake and the sake of Mother Beth. You mentioned that Ayita was proud of the fact that Harkahome was her adopted brother for saving her life but his true family is here in Kansas and this is where he belongs.

With all the work of the farm and my illness, Mother Beth and Father all but put the trial out of their minds. We were in town, getting supplies when Father picked up a newspaper that told of the ending of the trial of THE STATE VS. WILD HOG, ET AL.

The Prosecutor Mike Sutton failed to extradite any witnesses or survivors to Lawrence to prove that the correct Indians were on trial. It seems that Mr. Sutton was hastily married on October 1st and honeymooned until the 9th. The trial reconvened on the 13th with no provable case against the braves in custody. (It seems the love of a good woman can affect the outcome of many things!)

So, Little Hog, Noisy Walker, Blacksmith, Tangle Hair, Strong Left Hand, Old Crow and Porcupine were all held over for testimony on the conditions of the Darlington Agency that led to their people's exodus. The U.S. Senate Select Committee traveled to Lawrence to hear their story. They are, now, to be sent back to Darlington when they are done.

Mother Beth took the news very well, as you had explained to her, these were not the <u>young</u> braves that were responsible. The murderers never returned to the tribe, by all accounts of all the natives that you questioned.

So, my good husband, as far as your warming memory goes . . . I must tell you that I recall that picnic that you brought up. Did you know how upset I was that your sisters interrupted us and messed my hair? My mother took me away because I was on the verge of tears from it. I wanted to always be perfect and beautiful in your eyes and even though you tried to redo my hair, it and my dress were ruined by their playfulness. Mother could not calm me down. She took me to the buckboard and told me that you, William Clyde Lewis, loved me, regardless of the state of my hair. I could not believe that she said that. I could not believe that she knew that. She said that she, your mother and Grandmother Marilyn all knew of our feelings for each other. Then I was too embarrassed to stay at the picnic because OUR secret was exposed! I was such a silly little girl! I could have stayed at your side and enjoyed the rest of the afternoon with you!

So, I owe you a picnic, if truth be told. I cannot wait until you are by my side so we can lay in the spring grass and we can pick flowers for my hair. I cannot wait until you are by my side and we lay together. Period! These letters do allow us to say our true feelings with none of the blushing, getting in the way,

My health continues to improve, honest. I am keeping busy but at night, I worry and wonder where you are. I fall asleep thinking about you and only you. I think about you being next to me and holding me tight. When I wake up, my first thought is of your safety then I miss your morning kisses, hugs and touches. We did not get enough of those before you had to leave.

As the weather is getting colder here and where you are

going, please keep telling me more of your warming memories. Seeing them through your eyes and that big heart of yours, means so much to me. But do not dally in your mission, please. Come home to me with little Joshua and big Chilly. Give them both a big hug and then hug yourself for me.

Your devoted, loving wife who is missing you so much!!
Your Julia

THIRTY-SIX

November 17th, 1939
Friday in EL Dorado, cont'd

Matthew is back from class just in time for supper at the Johnson's farmhouse. During the meal, they fill him in on the contents of the safe. "Have you looked over the Will, yet? Is there anything irregular in that?"

They all look at one another. Helen answers, "Something very irregular. I am not sure that I understand or care for it but it is my father's dying wishes." She smiles at him. "I'm kidding! Papa thought this through, down to the very last detail. He didn't want me torn between Legacy Plantation and the Johnson Farms so he changed the trust so that," she pauses for dramatic effect. "Ahem! Judd Masters and his family will reside in the home and manage the estate as long, as they desire to do so!"

Matthew choked on his forkful. "Say that again?" He looks from Helen to Joshua to Eddie. "Is this a joke? What about Grand Mamá? Why would he give it to my Pa?"

Joshua answers, "The Will simply states, 'For services rendered above and beyond the normal measure by the man I consider a brother.' He has two codicils. Judd must allow Grand Mamá to continue to live here for long as she desires and he must keep the household staff on if *they* so desire. He left Grand Mamá ten thousand dollars and Sullivan and Mattie each five thousand dollars. Enough to live comfortably and have servants of their own, it seems." He looks at Sullivan who is standing at his place next to the sideboard. "Right, Sullivan?"

The man looks noticeably embarrassed. "That is what

Mistress Helen said. Iz don't want to leave here. Maw and me waz born here and we wants to continue to serve. Wouldn't be right to stay here and not serve. What would become of us?"

Matthew says, "Sullivan, my parents have never had servants. My Ma wouldn't know what to do with your Maw doing all the cooking."

Matilda comes out of the kitchen, in time to hear that. "Missus Judy is welcome in my kitchen any time. She is good folks. Twice she brought food and insisted on serving me and Sullivan. I 'member how she held my hand at Master Grant's good-bye. Missus Judy is as good a folk as there iz!"

Matthew is bewildered. "Does your Great Grandmother know?" He looks to Helen.

"Not yet. She has been out all day. I am going to offer her a home with us at Legacy Plantation. She lived in Lawrence before she was married but she is so active here, she might not want to travel back and forth. I will sit down with her as soon as she comes home. There is so much to tell her."

Matthew says, "I don't want to let Pa know until you've talked with her. She has every right to attest the will. This has been her home where she raised her family and you, Helen. She should have a say in this, don't you think?"

Helen shakes her head no and explains, "The home has never belonged to her, Matthew. She knows this. It has been in trust to each male heir but with my father being the last male born here, he had to change the trust. I assumed that the house would be mine but I am relieved that Judd will get it. If I am split between EL Dorado and Legacy both places will suffer. This way they will both flourish. Once the last of the Master's stops managing the estate, the property will revert, back to me and my heirs. Papa has thought of everything. It will just take some getting used to the notion.

Susan and Carolyn have been silent during the whole

discussion. They, also are confused and concerned by all the changes about to come. Carolyn says, "We still have to get Joshua off and Croner charged with Grant's murder. Any ideas?" She looks around the room.

Matthew says, "I think that I have one." He looks up at the man standing stoically at his station. "Sullivan, you'd recognize Croner, right? Would you mind giving us a hand with him?"

"What do you need me to do, Mister Matthew?"

Matthew turns to Eddie. "Call Byron, we need to plan this thoroughly. It might take some doing, but if we think it through, it just might work." He is smiling as he looks around to all those staring back at him. "We are going to set a trap for Croner, and Sullivan, if you assist us, you'll be the bait!!"

Sullivan smiles a very wide smile, "I'd be happy to be of service to you. Mister Matthew, it is my job, sir, to put *the trash* where it belongs." Everyone catches his pun and laughs. "Very happy, indeed, and un-e-quivic-ally!" He gives Eddie a nod and the gesture of tipping an invisible hat.

THIRTY-SEVEN

An Excerpt from Elizabeth Lewis's Journal
Wednesday, November 18, 1880 in Lawrence, Kansas

It took my Will and Chilly months of traveling to the area that was formally known as Dakota territory but is now the territory of Wyoming. Like a dog with a bone, he kept chewing at the miles, bit by bit. He arrived in the territorial capital, named Cheyenne (of all things) just after Thanksgiving last year. He telegrammed us at once of his whereabouts and we were again encouraged by his safe keeping but also by the rumor he had heard.

About a hundred miles north of the capital is a mixed tribe of Cheyenne and Lakota Indians that have a yellow haired teacher and her white-man's son called Harkahome. Will thinks that Lydia is alive and living with this band of mixed tribe Indians.

I prayed that it was so and that he can get them away from the hardships of those people and back to the warmth and safety of Lawrence. He later wrote that once women are accepted into a tribe, as proven by giving her the honor of teacher, the tribe generally do not want them to leave. I know he was bracing me for disappointment.

Will and Chilly were going to wait a few days for a break in the snowy weather before heading back out for the next arduous trek. I cannot imagine the fortitude that my two sons have for remaining true to their mission, no matter their own personal suffering. Bound and determined were they and here is proof!

Just as their horses were packed and ready to go, that late November, Will, slipped down a snowy set of stairs and broke his ankle. The doctor said that he must not put weight on it for six to eight weeks. The weather will be most severe by then but he refused to give up. He said that as soon as he can stand without pain, he will proceed with his mission. They were back on their horses by the first week of December.

Here in Lawrence, we were putting the farm to bed, as we call the late fall time. Again, much work to do for all the tilling and plotting of next year's crops take place before our winter snows fall.

Julia has flourished since her procedure and being reunited with Will for that brief time. She was so happy to receive his telegram for she had a small box of letters to send him and he did stay in Cheyenne long enough to receive them. I know that she is praying on the safe return of Lydia, Joshua, Chilly and most of all her beloved Will.

An Excerpt from the letters of
Julia Lewis

November 30, 1879

My Dearest Will,

    Please receive this small bundle of letters from me as proof of my unwavering love for you. We said that we would write a letter each week and I am trying to fulfil my end of the bargain.

    The most wonderful news of Lydia's existence is an unasked prayer come true. Didn't Ayita or Nokomis ever intimate that Harkahome had a yellow haired mother? I find that more than frustrating. You might have used that information to have the pair stand out even more than just a small white-man's boy. A scout or rumor might have surfaced much sooner if the truer image of your search was known.

    I sense that this is the final leg of your mission and that you will return to me with all haste. It has been so long again that I am beginning to feel like I have made you up in my dreams. Then I will reread one of your letters and clutch the proof of your existence to my bosom. If not for your endearing letters, I would have given up long ago. Not on you but on my foolish imagination thinking we were a dream of love that only exists in a fairy tales.

    I am being so foolish and I hope that you hold all my foolishness against me. Hold all of yourself against me. Be at my side and never stray again, my love. I could not bear it!

    Mother Beth has taken the news of Lydia's living with the Cheyenne with a grain of salt. She is relieved that she survived but concerned that she will not see Lydia or Joshua ever again. She wants you to let Lydia know that she is loved and welcomed back with open arms. Beg Lydia to come back to her. She cannot wait to give her a big hug and one to her grandson.

    Speaking of hugs, I could use one right now from my favorite fellow. Tell Chilly I am sending him one right now.

    As for you my favorite Husband . . . I am to be so bold and send you only a whisper of my love for I am saving the rest for when you get home from your arduous journey.

I plan on showering you with kisses and hugs and touches and you will barely survive what I have planned for you. I promise you. My health has so greatly improved and we will be able to thoroughly enjoy all the pleasures of our marriage bed, like we have never done before!

So, come home to me, my Husband. Let me look in your eyes and feel your touch and know that I will never be part from you again!

Your no longer patiently waiting wife
Forever yours,

Julia

An excerpt of the letters of
Colonel William Lewis

December 5th, 1879

Dearest Darling Impatient Wife,

You do not have very much longer. I am headed out to the Cheyenne/Lakota band, tomorrow morning at first light. As I said in my telegram, I had a small set-back, in our departure but my ankle has stopped paining me enough to get on a horse. It will be thoroughly healed before we reach their encampment, do not fear.

The break was destined by the Almighty, himself, for it allowed me to receive my Love's letters and gave me time to thoroughly read each one.

I am so glad that you've taken to writing so often, I feel that I have been so remiss in this area, especially since you've depended on my words on paper as a stand-in for proof of our love. You should be showered by my letters as well as kisses, hugs and touches!

I wish that I had time to respond to each letter in full but my journey must be started, if it is to ever be finished. I want it to end so that we have the family together and whole again. I want us to be together and whole again.

In all the time that we have been writing to each other, you have never shared your day to day small doings like you finally have in the bundled letters. Please continue to do so for I feel like I am still there, watching you daily. It brings such gladness to my heart that my home has been your home and that it is natural for it to be so.

As soon as I return, though, I plan on building us a little home not far from the farm but not on the property like Ian and Grandfather Clyde's homes are. I know that I will be the one inheriting the farm someday since Joseph is a doctor in Wichita and Chilly has no interest in it.

We have talked about it at great length for there is little else to talk about. He is dead set against being a farmer and will join the army as soon as we arrive home. Please do not let Mother know, he might change his mind, or I might change it for him.

I want to be the farmer. I always did want that but I was hurting so and needed to be useful on a grander scale to forget my pain. That is why I joined the army. It was that or admit my glaring horrendous mistake of letting you leave!

Please do not let me be so pig-headed like that again! This will be your most sacred duty. Do not let me leave you, ever again! My heart will not be able to take it! And I might do something foolish like join the army again! Just kidding!

My army life and traveling life are finished with this last journey that is not directly home. Even if this is a false lead, I think that I will be done looking for them. I cannot be away from you any longer, either.

So, pray that it is truly them and that I will be able to escort them home, without difficulty. Pray that the weather will hold out for us and that I am home in time for the Holidays!

Home for the Holidays might not be possible with all the distance I need to cover on our way home, but I plan on selling the horses and taking trains and stage coaches for they are so much faster!

Home for the Holidays, makes me think of a warming memory! This one goes way back. Chilly was only two I think, so, you were living in Lawrence for two years already. We had all opened our presents together and the grown-ups were either cooking or talking in the parlor.

You and my little sisters received beautiful baby dolls from

Grandmother Marilyn and were playing Mommy with them. I had been given a sling shot and a wooden gun. I could not wait to get with my friends and work on our expertise with them. But on Christmas Day, they were with their own family and I was watching you teach my sisters how to hold their dollies and feed them.

I suddenly pictured you as my wife and feeding our little one. I was already so in love with you, that I daydreamed of you often, but this time I could see the adult you in a kitchen making my meal, and making my home the place that I would never want to leave. I just sat there until you asked me to stop staring at you. I was looking your way but I was staring with my mind's eye into the future. I was so embarrassed, as if you <u>had</u> read my thoughts. I got off the sofa and came to you and whispered something to you. Do you recall what that was? It was a question and you remained silent in front of everyone but your smile answered it. That was my best Christmas Present, ever!

Why did I waste all those years apart? Why was I so stubborn as to not remember all those daydreams that are still my dreams, today!

That is why I will build you the best house I can as another symbol of my unending love for you. I Promise that I will also <u>keep</u> building homes for you to affirm that our lives and love will only increase with each passing year.

During the long silences of my travels, I will be thinking of the house plans and I will have the first house all built in my mind before we meet again. Then we will live in it and many others

Happily, Ever After!

Yours to have forever,
Your Will

THIRTY-EIGHT

November 18th, 1939
Saturday in EL Dorado, Kansas

It has been decided that on Monday, the trap will be set into motion. They have met with Byron Brewster's men and have a detailed report on Albert Croner's comings and goings. They will continue the surveillance until he is behind bars.

Tonight, however, there is to be a big party at Melinda and Mark's house to celebrate their 3rd Wedding Anniversary. The actual date is the 21st but since that is a Tuesday, the couple wanted to celebrate the event on the weekend so everyone can attend.

Susan and Matthew have not told Judd and Judy about Grant's will, just yet. They are waiting for Helen herself to do it, when the time is right. Matthew is hoping that the time will be tonight.

Henry, Frank, Anna and Clara Beth come in from Lawrence, again, with mail and come directly to the Johnson farmhouse to deliver it. Henry needs to talk with Joshua for a time about dealings on the farm.

Mattie meets them at the door because she loves children. Little Clara Beth exclaims delight at seeing Carolyn, Joshua and Helen. Mattie rushes to her and bends down to the child and says, "Oh, Mattie iz so happy to meet you, Clara Beth, I hearz so many things 'bout you. Do you want to come into Mattie's kitchen? I have fresh baked cookies coming out of the oven, cuz I hear'd you were coming!" Clara is torn between going for a cookie or staying with the adults she knows and loves. She looks to her Mama for a decision.

"You can go with Matilda, Clara. When you finish your cookie, she will bring you to us, I promise." Anna pats her head and gives her a little push of encouragement in Matilda's direction. That is all she needed and she is hand in hand with Matilda and skipping to the cookies.

Carolyn watches her go. "She has grown overnight. This is

the one thing that I don't like about being in EL Dorado. No Harrick family members around!" She hugs her sister Anna.

Anna gives her a squeeze back. "Well, the main house is horrible without the Lewis family in it!"

Matilda has a light lunch prepared and during the meal, Joshua fills them in on Grant's note to Helen and the 'plan'. No one mentions the Will or it's beneficiaries.

As soon as the meal is over, the women help Matilda clear the table and do the dishes. Anna says, "I wish we could stay longer but I promised Melinda and Ma that I would help with the cooking."

As she starts to leave the kitchen, Helen calls Anna to stop. She goes to her and quietly asks. "You are going to continue my lessons, aren't you?" Anna nods. Helen continues. "I was hoping that you'd say that. I cannot wait until we get home so I can start again. The first thing I want to learn is Joshua's favorite meal. Your meatloaf. Can we make that first?"

"Absolutely! I cannot wait until all this nonsense is over and I have you all home again. It is very lonely, just us three." Anna gives her a hug. "I miss both my sisters, very much."

Helen just beams.

***

They are all gathered after a wonderful meal in the parlor of Melinda and Mark's house. The room is full, and it is standing room only. Melinda's bosses, Joan and Petro are there, as well as the Lewis family, including Great Grand Mamá, the James family, the Harrick family and of course all of the Masters family. Many have little gifts for the happy couple and they are opening them. Afterward, Mark and his glowing wife, Melinda, thank everyone for coming.

When they are done and everyone is talking at once, Helen and Joshua stand and face everyone.

Joshua give a little "Ahem!" and they all stop to look at him. "My Helen has a little announcement that will be of great interest to many of you present."

Helen blushes and begins. "I know that the presents were

all for the Happy Couple but I have a present for Judd Masters and his family. Judd and Judy, can you come to us please?"

The older couple get up from the couch and cross the room and stand by the Lewis couple. "What is going on?" asks Judd.

"Well, Judd, you know that my father held you in the highest regards. You are a man of integrity, hardworking, and very dedicated to the farm. My father wanted to give you a gift." She holds out a small box for Judd to take. "This is for you and your wife and for your family."

"In that little box? What could it be?" He asks. He reaches for it and shakes it. It makes no sound so he hands it to Judy. "You do the honors, my dear, you love a surprise more than me."

Judy takes the box from him and takes the cover off it. She reaches in and pulls out a single key. She holds it up so that everyone can see it. "A key? I don't understand. What is it a key to?" She looks at Helen.

"My father wants the Masters to have the Johnson Estates Farmhouse. As long, as you manage the farm business, you will have a roof over your head."

Judy is still confused. "What farmhouse?"

"The one I was born in, and raised as were the six generations before me. The one that you've delivered meals to twice since my Papa's passing."

Judy looks to Grand Mamá. "Isn't that your home since you were a newlywed. Why would we take it from you?" Judy is starting to tear up.

Grand Mamá stands and goes to her. "I will be moving in with Helen and Joshua. I would like to keep my bedroom in the house when I need to come to town for meetings and other activities. That is one of the terms of the will. I get to stay for as long, as I like. Also, Mattie and Sullivan get to stay for as long, as they like. Grant very generously gave them each a large inheritance but they both want to stay living there and working. Mattie is getting on in years and will need to slow down soon, but she says that she will be honored to share a kitchen with you, Judy. I must say, you won her over, thoroughly, when you brought food and held her hand at the services. She loves you."

"I don't know what to say!" Judy is waving a hand in front of herself to cool off. "Is it warm in here? I think I need to sit down." Judd takes her back to the couch.

"What about you Helen?" Judd asks. "Don't you want to continue to live in EL Dorado? Like you said, it's been in your family for generations."

"And it is <u>still</u> in my family. When you retire, if Matthew, Mark or Henry no longer manages the business, the house reverts to me and my heirs. Papa wanted to make sure that I wasn't torn between EL Dorado and Lawrence. With you in charge of everything, I can rest easy. I will expect those monthly reports that you prepared for Papa, but not much else hands on."

"Well, blow me down with a feather! Pa, you are moving up in the world!" Melinda says. "When do y'all move in?"

THIRTY-NINE

November 20ᵗʰ, 1939
Monday in EL Dorado, Kansas

Sullivan is wired up and waiting outside the Kettle Diner at eight in the morning. There is a sign in the window that says 'COFFEE and a Fresh Made DOUGHNUT – 15¢'. He has his large hand on the door handle but looks around. The car across the street is one from Brewster's Detective Agency. Inside the diner are its two former occupants, sitting at a table. Sullivan enters and sees a sign by the register that says 'Coloreds – TO GO service, only – No exceptions'. He sees the man he came to see, sipping a cup of coffee.

Croner looks at the man. Sullivan looks back at him and nods, holding his hat in his hand, nervously. He doesn't smile. After the counter girl takes his order and brings him a coffee to go. Sullivan asks Croner, "Could you pass me the sugar, Mr. Croner, please."

Though he was surprised that the man knew his name, he doesn't give him a second look, he just slides the sugar across to him.

"Much obliged, sir." Sullivan fixes his coffee with sugar and cream. "It's a mighty cool day out, isn't it? Mr. Croner?"

Croner finally turns to him. "Do I know you?"

"Yes, sir, I iz Grant Johnson's man. You came to the Farmhouse and paid him a visit a time or two."

"Oh yes. Samuel, isn't it?" He chuckles to himself and looks forward again.

"No, sir. It's Sullivan, sir. I 'member you. Especially since I saw you the night Mr. Grant was killed."

"I don't know what you are talking about." He says with his eyes still looking forward.

Sullivan moves much closer to Croner, and says in a voice very low. "You'd better know'd what I am talking 'bout or I will be talking to the police. Iz heard you arguing in the study, then Iz saw you outside with Mr. Grant."

197

"If you did, why didn't you tell that to the cops? They have someone else charged with his murder."

"I figured, by waitin', I would be able to have some of that $2500 that you took from Master Grant that night."

Croner turns to him with his jaw set in anger, but whispers. "Why, you no-good nigger, how dare you accuse a white man. For all I know, you did it."

Sullivan keeps calm and gives Croner a hint of a smile. He whispers back. "Well, sir, Iz weren't the one helping Master Grant with hiz headaches in that house, now, wuz I? You see, the ways Iz figures it, you made plenty of money over the years, but if you wants to spend any of that payout, you'd better share some. Iz ain't asking much, just $500! That's only a fifth of it as Iz can cipher it. Call it a forgetter's fee, instead of a finder's fee. Get it? Sir?" Sullivan elbows Croner and smiles completely now as his white teeth are bright in the dim light.

"Well, I don't have that kind of cash on me. We'd have to meet somewhere. Give me a day or two days and . . ." He stops for Sullivan's large black hand is on his forearm, squeezing it.

"You - do not have two days, sir. I want it today! I cannot stand that house no more now that Master Grant is gone and as Iz sees it, you ain't got nothing important doing today, anyway."

"You expect me to just get you $500? How do I know that you won't turn me in, anyway?"

"You don't." He pauses "I knowz that Master Grant wanted to die before hiz headaches got worse. May he rest in peace. But I also knowz that he didn't want to do it with hiz Juliet Helen home. He told you to not to come around and he tried to get you to leave. You argued with him, stole the money outta the tin and hiz gun then you took him into the woods, and you done shot him. It were a great idea to go to Mister Joshua and hit him on the head, steal his car and leave the Navy colt gun in it. If Iz didn't see you walk to the woods that night, I would have believed HE'd done it. I have to hand it to you, Mr. Croner – that wuz purty smart. Do you believe me that I knowz you were the one who done it?"

Croner just nods.

"Iz didn't hear you, Mr. Croner. Iz a little slight of hearing. Do you believe that I knowz you're the one who killed Master?"

"Yes, damn it, Sullivan! Now keep your voice down and let's get out of here."

"I'd be happy to, sir, now that we'z come to an 'understandin'. Now, let's go to your Citizens State Bank for my money. I'll pay for breakfast." He pulls out a dollar and leaves it on the table and calls out. "Miss, this iz for the both of us."

Once outside together, Sullivan puts his hand on Croner's arm again. "Mr. Croner, if you'd be so kind as to drive, we'll get there mighty quick."

It is a short ride to the Bank. Croner and Sullivan do not talk. Croner gets out of the car and Sullivan does the same. He has his hand on Croner's arm again. "Iz will go in with you, but Iz will stay by the door. Bring me the full amount, got it?"

"Yes, yes, I got it." Croner goes to the center table and takes a withdrawal slip from one of the under-the-table pockets and scribbles on it quickly. He goes to his favorite teller and, without saying anything, hands it to her.

She looks at it and opens her drawer. "Do you want any of that in big bills, sir?" She doesn't make eye contact. Croner turns to look at Sullivan, who shakes his head no.

"Just twenties will be fine." He says, "Be quick about it."

"Yes, sir, right away." She counts quietly to herself then turns the stack over and counts it out loud to Croner. When she is done, she says, "Did you want an envelope for this, sir?"

"Yes. Hurry, I haven't got all day."

She hands him the envelope and looks at the next person in line, behind him. "Next!" She says, just a little too loud.

Croner puts the envelope in his pocket, and when he gets to Sullivan, he says, "Can't we talk about this?"

"We can talk, but let's get outzide." They leave the bank and Sullivan walks him to a bench, just out front. "Now hand me the money and you won't have to worry about me, no more."

"This will be the only time I give you anything. I refuse to be blackmailed any further, do you hear me? You will never bring up Grant's murder again. Right?" He hands the envelope to Sullivan. Sullivan opens it and looks at all the cash.

"Oh, Iz hearz you Mr. Croner, so does Mr. Pollock from the States Attorney's office. I don't have to mention the murder, no more. You said it real loud, yourself. Hah! You just hung yourself!" Sullivan has his hand on Croner's arm again with a smile, a mile wide, then easily brings him to a standing position. When the two men from the Brewster's Agency come from behind and each grab an arm, Sullivan steps back.

Croner looks over both men holding him. "Which one of you is Mr. Pollock? You have his word against mine here." Both men shake their heads.

Matthew walks up from behind the Bank with his friend Anthony Pollock. They approach Croner. Matthew says to the ADA, "Don't you think paying for 'hush money' is as a good a confession as there is? I do!"

"What are you doing here, Punk?" Croner says, calling him the name that he always used in the fields for the trouble maker.

"Getting justice for Joshua, my brother. Let me introduce you to Anthony Pollock, the Assistant District Attorney, he is an old friend of mine. Mr. Pollock, meet Grant Johnson's killer!"

FORTY

An Excerpt from Elizabeth Lewis's Journal
Friday November 20, 1880 in Lawrence

Will prepared me for the news but it still hit me and knocked me down and crushed the breath out of my lungs. My William said that he thought that I'd collapse, completely by the look of me.

We received the news via a telegram saying that a detailed letter will follow shortly. I did not know if I could comprehend a detailed letter. This was too much to take in.

Will and Chilly did reach the Camp of the mixed tribe in Wyoming without further delay. He and Chilly and their scouts approached the camp on foot and without guns. I shudder to think of it.

Will, of course, was still limping, according, to Chilly's account of it all. They immediately stated the reason for their arrival, the search for their kinsmen, now known as Harkahome and his yellow haired mother.

They were briskly ushered to a teepee and a guard was put on them while the scouts outside explained their mission, further

It took a better part of the day, until someone entered the teepee. It was Joshua Nathaniel with his hair all grown out and in the Indian fashion of hanging at his shoulders. He wore Indian trousers as he must have outgrown everything he was wearing. He turned twelve in May and he was some five foot - five inches already. But they recognized him and Joshua knew his Uncles. He ran to Chilly and jumped into his arms, and Chilly held him and hugged him for a long time. Finally, Will had to say, "Don't I get a hug, too?" This broke the spell and Joshua turned to Will and held out his hand. Will said he looked down on that hand, grabbed it and pulled him into a hug - so tight!

I am crying at the wonderful image. That I could have been a part of it! I would have smothered that boy even if he is taller than me now. No sooner than they let go of each other, questions were being asked by all parties but no one had time to answer before Lydia walked into the teepee. Her yellow hair was longer and down in braids. She wore a buckskin squaw's dress and moccasins. She had beads around her neck which meant she has an elder in good standing in the tribe. Will said that when he saw the beads, he knew it would be a futile trip to try to bring them home.

She smiled and went to each of her brothers-in-law and gave them a good hug. She was crying, the whole time.

She told them of how they survived the massacre. She never knew how many settlers were killed, and was appalled at the number. She told them so much that I will just include her letter to me that explains it all.

The Letter from Lydia Stone Lewis

December, 1879

My Dearest Mother,

By now you have heard that Joshua Nathaniel and I escaped the tragedy at Oberlin. How you must have grieved for us and I had no way to lighten your load with the news of our survival. I have called out to you in my heart, in my sleep and in the light of day, hoping that you would hear me and know in your heart that we are safe and dare I say content with the life that we now live. Please do not hate me for it. I have feared that the news of our death had caused you a fatal blow and I am so relieved to know that you are well, despite your grief.

Let me explain the events that have brought me to this life:

Ian and I were given a party in Oberlin on our arrival with the herd of 200 cattle. It was a long dry trip and we enjoyed that party more than I can tell you. Everyone was so thankful that we made the trip in a shorter time than expected and we feasted and danced and drank. That is my last happy memory of my Ian. He felt ten feet tall that night, with the hero's welcome and praise given him.

The following two days were rugged as the new settlers were being trained on handling the herd. I barely saw Ian for he was gone before sun-up and worked late into the night. I brought him meals and felt his presence beside me in bed but we had no time for conversations. He wanted to be able to leave within the next two days and he complained that the men who were being trained needed three weeks to understand cattle.

We didn't have three weeks or two days as it turned out. The next day, our fourth day there, the Cheyenne came. Oberlin only had about sixty people among all the families but the number of Cheyenne braves seemed double that. Like

203

Quantrill's men, they seemed to wash in over us like an unexpected wave. They were everywhere at once.

I was with the women in the community kitchen, baking and we were laughing at the antics of their foolish husbands trying to be cowhands, when the shots started. I ran out to find Joshua and saw the body of my husband. I do not know how or when my Ian died. I saw his lifeless body just outside the cattle gate. I could not go to him for the cattle were still stampeding through the street. I went behind the house and found the lot that Joshua was playing in. There was a very young brave (Joshua's age) there trying to protect his little sister. She was headed into the path of the cattle. A settler, Mr. Callahan, came out of nowhere with his shotgun and aimed for the brave and his little sister. Joshua ran to him and knocked the shotgun to the ground and Mr. Callahan slapped Joshua so hard that he fell down. The settler retrieved his gun and took aim again but this time a bullet stopped him. He was shot by the father of the young brave.

I ran to Joshua and I stood there trying to shield him from being shot and expecting to die, there. The young boy came to us and put his sister in my arms and took Joshua's hand and led us to horses. We all got on them and rode out together. It all happened so fast. I don't think it was fifteen minutes from the first shot to us on the run!

At first Joshua and I begged to be released. He was bruised and we were not used to riding bareback. They did not seem to understand my words. My tears did seem to affect them, and they treated us with kindness despite our captivity. We were so isolated with the tribe that I knew I we tried to escape we would perish in the elements for winter came early that year.

It was the family of the boy brave that took us in. Joshua Nathaniel, by saving the lives of two Cheyenne was owed two lives and that is why they took us. Degotoga is the boy brave and Ayita is his little sister. They had an older brother named Mantotohpa. Kanuna is the father and Nokomis is his second wife. They gave the name Harkahome to Joshua. I am called Ja-une or Yellow squaw. Degotoga and Harkahome are now sworn blood brothers, a very serious title and honor with the Cheyenne.

We were on the run for months, never stopping in one place for more than a night. The Winter was indescribably cold. I do not know how we survived it. Kanuna and Nokimis fought over which chief to follow when Little Wolf and Dull Knife split paths, so she took her son Matotohpa and daughter Ayita with her to follow Dull Knife, her kinsman. Kanuna was left adrift himself when his wife Nokomis disobeyed him, took his oldest son and little girl from him . Though, through her actions SHE was dead to him, he mourned the loss of her anyway. He was devastated by the loss of his children. These proud people revere their young and old alike.

Kanuna stayed with Little Wolf for a time but had Lakota family with his late first wife and we left Little Wolf and tried to locate them. It took us months until we were successful. They were very long months but Kanuna led many of the Kansas Cheyenne to this tribe of Lakota's that we now call family.

I grieved for my husband, Ian, and felt lost without the man who loved me so dearly. I loved your son so much. I am still devastated that he is gone, but I had to go on living for Harkahome's sake. Yes, I call him that now that I am the third wife of Kanuna. There I said it and I am sure that you wish that I had died before I dishonored your son in this fashion. But it wasn't like that.

Kanuna saved my life and had no part in the killing of the other settlers. He was just trying to get his children out of the way of danger from Mr. Callahan and the cattle. Mother, they were so hungry!! Even after they cooked and cured the meat, they were starving.

Kanuna has protected me with his life on multiple occasions from other tribesman as well as coyote and a bear. Yes, he fought a Bear for me and won! He took wounds that I did not think he could survive but he did. He never forced himself on me, Mother. He was kind and gentle and I started to accept and appreciate the man, his people and the way of life that they were willing to die to protect.

I have other news for you as well. With all my hardships of traveling and just trying to survive, after Kanuna took me for his wife, I became pregnant and gave birth to a beautiful son that we named Avonaco. I had all those miscarriages, one after the other in Lawrence. I still cannot believe that here on the move, barely eating and always looking over our shoulders, I conceived and carried a healthy boy to term!

So now I am Cheyenne and so are my two sons, and though I know that you would not be different to us because of it, Lawrence would. So, we are content with this life and though I miss you and Lawrence, I do not feel a need to come back. I am no longer a white woman. I am proud of my journey of survival, and my long trek. I had my losses, too. As you once put it, the losses weighed heavily upon me and my husband sought to comfort me.

I do hope that you can forgive me and do not think that I sought this way of life. I have just tried to survive as I must for my boys.

I am keeping Lawrence and Ian alive in Harkahome's heart so that one day, he might want to see how the other half still lives. He talks of you, his Gram Beth, and Chilly all the time. I have continued to teach him to read and write and I have taught Degotoga and a few others as well. Joshua is happy here with his blood brother, Degotoga. They are just as close as he and Chilly were, if you can believe that!

I am so very grateful that Will has been searching for Joshua Nathaniel for all this time. I am forever in his debt for leaving his new wife and home for all these months to find him. The winter in these parts are so cruel and even with his broken ankle, my brother Navoualevé was not deterred. We Cheyenne have a great respect for him and all that he has done for OUR people. He said he did not know that I survived. He thought that only Joshua did and that he started out seeking justice for Joshua but there is no need for that. Joshua has been given a great gift and honor, among these people. He is learning to know, understand and love another culture. This education cannot be bought. Chilly and Harkahome have rekindled their friendship and dare I say Chilly gained a friend with Degotoga.

Will was insisting that I leave with him but I cannot take my son Avonaco with me for Cheyenne do not allow male sons to be raised outside of the tribe and I could not let my first born leave a family that he has come to love as much as the one he had for the first twelve years of his life. I also cannot leave my husband, for I do love this man, Kanuna. He is now my home as much as Ian was my home in Lawrence.

Please forgive me and keep us forever in your prayers,

Your daughter still in my heart.
Ja-une formally known as Lydia Stone Lewis

CHERISSE M HAVLICEK

An Excerpt for the Letters of
Colonel William Lewis

December 18, 1879

My Dearest Darling Wife,

As I said in the telegram, we are headed home. My mission is completed. I have found my nephew and his mother, they are safe and sound and I do believe happy.

It is my great sadness that they do not want to come back with us. They said that they might come back at some time in the future, for a visit but from what I know of the Indian culture, they do not take what we call vacations. It was very sad to leave them. Even Chilly, for all his bravado, wept. He was leaving his childhood best friend. I know that pain, all too well.

But now I am on my way home to that best friend, now my dearest wife. I will be that farmer that tills his land and watches good things grow. I will be an active member in my community and church. I will host balls and parties, so that I can make up for all the dances we have missed out on. I will take you on those picnics and long walks and put flowers in your hair again. I will be all the things that I have dreamed of, so often.

I do have that house built in my mind's eye, it will be a simple one for all these trips have been a drain on our finances but it will do splendidly for the first of our many homes, that I will build for you.

But first, you and I will go away, immediately, upon my return for a second honeymoon. I want you all to myself, to have and to hold and to lay with. I will take you up on your offer to use me as you have never done before!

God, I hope no one else ever reads these letters! Proprieties be damned!!! I want to make love to you so bad and so often that neither of us will be able to ride a horse!

I will leave you shocked by my words and pray that you are to be my very willing partner in this endeavor.

Oh, did you recall that question, I asked you on that Christmas morning? I asked you to marry me, so I am thinking that your leaving was your broken promise of a future not mine! Remind me to hold that against you, later!

Your devoted and 'soon to be never parted from'
Loving Husband,

Your Will.

An Excerpt from the Letters of
Julia Lewis

December 22 1879

My Dearest Darling Husband,

Your letter just arrived in Lawrence and I fear that you will not be here for the Holidays as you planned. But whenever you arrive, it will be the cause of the biggest Celebration!!

Your last letter left me shocked, speechless and with breathing difficulties. To write down all that you imagine doing is beyond proper.

But, PROPRIETIES BE DAMNED!

I await your homecoming. I await your touch, your kisses, your hugs, your making love to me so much that neither of us will be able to ride a horse! I am saying yes to it all!

Hurry my darling, for I cannot start without you. Fly home to me so that you are mine forever and we will live

Happily, Ever After!

Your loving wife and slave to wanting you,

Julia

FORTY-ONE

November 23rd, 1939
Thanksgiving Day in EL Dorado

Last Monday, after the trap was sprung, the sheriff's police arrived to take Albert Croner and book him for the murder of Grant Johnson. Curtis Miles immediately called for a dismissal of the case against Joshua Lewis, and with the testimony of ADA Pollock, it is granted.

The Brewster Agency hands over all their notes of their surveillance to the new prosecuting attorney. The next day, the incriminating evidence of payments to Acron Dry Goods and Grant's note to Helen is turned over as well. The prosecutor was thrilled to have more than half of his work done for him.

The Thanksgiving Day meal is at the Johnson Farmhouse. Judy and Judd come to the house just after sun-up so Judy can prepare the meal. Mattie is just thrilled working in the kitchen with her.

Helen is just amazed because Matilda never allowed her to help, or even eat in the kitchen. She always said that it wasn't right for her to be like the hired help. Helen tried to kid her about her turnabout thinking, but Mattie replied, "I am an Inheritor now, same as iz Missus Judy. We iz equals in this house. I'z don't work for them and they don't need me to work for them, neither!" That logic just left Helen to shake her head.

The house is the fullest it has been since her Wedding and like that time, smiles and congratulations are shared all around.

After the huge three p.m. Thanksgiving feast all the men retire to the front parlor to smoke congratulatory cigars and discuss the new state, of affairs.

Joshua says, "Helen plans on packing up her father's bedroom in a few weeks. She wants to spend some time in Lawrence, first. It surprises me that she is excited about this shift in tenants. I am very proud of her. From the way, she is talking, you should be able to move in before the Holidays."

Judd looks concerned. "We are not in any hurry, Joshua. I hope she knows this. I still do not feel right being in a house that was in her family for so very long."

"Think of it as you are being our place holder. I want a large family and someday, this will be an inheritance for them. I was thinking of buying another farm somewhere half way between here and Lawrence so that I have a house and farm to leave to each child we have!

"Do you, now?" Helen is standing in the parlor doorway with her hands on her hips. "Don't think you should have discussed this with your wife? Who do you think is going to be birthing all these babies?"

"Gram Beth's great, great granddaughter! She had eight babies, now I don't think we should go that far, but the sky is the limit!" He crosses to her and gives her a squeeze. "Or we could just love this one, either way, I am the luckiest man alive!"

"Hear, Hear!" They all cheer.

FORTY-TWO

An Excerpt from Elizabeth Lewis's Journal
November 25, 1880
Thanksgiving Day in Lawrence

I was still reeling from Will's disheartening telegram and the letter that followed to enjoy last year's Christmas Holidays. Mother Marilyn and Julia and my girls all pitched in and cooked and cleaned and decorated, while I took to my bed. I hurt so bad from the loss of my son and his family, even though I knew Lydia and Joshua were safe and happy; they were lost to me, none-the-less.

Our household was all excited for this would be the first time that my Wichita doctors, Joseph and Lizzie will be home for the Holidays. Joseph and his wife, Katherine are bringing their newborn son, Samuel, for us to meet. I am so relieved that life goes on but I did not want to partake of it at the same time. It was that damn grayness that looms over all that could be good in my life.

We had just finished our Christmas Dinner and were sitting full beyond measure when there was a commotion on the porch. My heart leapt for joy when a few seconds later, Will and Chilly burst in like wild men! The uproar that it started!! Tears were shed all around.

I can still see Julia's expression as she came out of the kitchen at the sound of the ruckus. Surprise and delight do not begin to convey the glow that she radiated! She cried out his name and ran to him and he to her. Once again, he held her at arms-length, looked her up and down and cried out, "Luckiest man alive!", before he bent down and slowly kissed her. Then he picked her up and swung her all around!!

We had such a good week with my whole family together again. The only dull spot was the loss of Ian's family, but we included them in our toasts and our prayers and our memories. My William said that if we continue to do this, they are never, *really, gone.*

After the New Year, after my Wichita family members were on their way home, Will took his Julia away for that long second honeymoon, he promised.

When they came back home, he started buying the supplies needed to build his house. He hadn't even closed the deal on the land that he wanted, yet. He was that sure of his plans.

William and Will started planning the new year's crop schedule to include the soon-to-be-owned adjoining land. They also planned to buy more calves to raise. Will jumped into farming with both feet, and as if he had never been gone.

So, I have come to the end of my tale of my losses and why I have not written for so long. Seeing it all written out does let sunlight break through all the gray.

But watching Julia's Will come back and keep all his promises to her has helped me even more. I take comfort that my eldest son's tragedy has brought my Will, his Julia.

Will has been good to his word to her and built an adorable little house on that land he acquired. They have gone on numerous picnics - just the two of them. He also has kept his word as far as dances are concerned. He has already rented out the ballroom of the newly constructed Lawrence Hotel for two Balls - one last Easter and one on May Day. Tomorrow night is his third Ball. This one is for Thanksgiving.

I know that he and Julia will dance every dance, together. And, although he will be the host, he will ignore everyone else, again. For there are never any other people in the room when Colonel William Clyde Lewis has his Julia in his arms.

And I see it all in beautiful living color and not the pencil drawings of my grief filled eyes.

FORTY-THREE

November 28th, 1939
Tuesday in Lawrence, Kansas

Everyone is back home in Lawrence. Anna is at the main house at her usual time, putting the coffee on for Carolyn and the tea kettle on for Juliet Helen. Anna had spent the last two days catching up on the journals and love letters between the Colonel and his Julia. She is so happy that she is part of this wonderful family. The Colonel was such a wonderful loving man with the biggest heart that didn't shrink when his outside appearance did. After putting on the morning drinks, she goes to pet Robbie, the Colonel's old dog laying in his bed under the sink. She picks up the old guy and gives him a hug. Henry walks in and catches her with a tear in her eye.

"Anna, what's going on? I don't think I should have let you read the Colonel's letters, they have gotten you so glum."

Anna stands up and wipes her eyes. "They are happy tears, my love. I feel so proud of the Colonel and so happy for him that he is with his Julia dancing in Heaven." Even though she says she is happy, she runs to him to cry on his shoulder.

Joshua and Helen enter the room. "What's all this?" Joshua asks the couple. "Anna are you feeling alright?" He goes to them. "Henry, is she ill?"

Henry just smiles at Joshua. "No, she just loves the Colonel so very much. She is very sensitive about him, and just finished the journal entries and love letters." He turns back to his wife. "Come now, Anna. Quit this nonsense, we have breakfast to cook and chores to do!"

Helen adds, "You don't want to get fired, do you?"

Anna looks up at that in shock, but even though Helen is smiling, Helen says. "I am being serious, now, Anna."

Carolyn and Eddie enter the kitchen. Carolyn goes straight to the coffee. "What's going on here? Eddie needs his breakfast. He starts back at the University this morning at

215

ten!" She turns to look at the other two women who are still looking intently at each other.

Helen says, "I asked you a question, Anna. Do you want to be fired?"

Anna looks at her. "I don't understand, Helen, why would you fire me? Are you pulling my leg?"

"No, not at all. I have been thinking about this for quite some time and well, now that you've shown me how to make my husband's favorite meal, I think that your services are no longer required, here."

Carolyn steps in. "Now, just a minute Helen, one meatloaf dinner doesn't mean we don't need or want Anna here! This is her home."

Helen puts her hand up to silence her sister-in-law. "Carolyn, Joshua and I discussed this last night as husbands and wives do. We have made up our minds."

All eyes turn to Joshua. "It will make my Helen very happy so I agree with her."

This makes Anna turn white and looks like she might faint. Helen softens, "Please sit down, Anna. You don't look so good."

Henry takes Anna to a seat. He is very upset about this conversation, and can't hold his tongue, any longer. "Why are you doing this to her? She has never done anything to you!"

Helen sticks her chin out. "Yes she has! She has shown me what it is to be strong and humble, despite adversity; how to be loving, thoughtful and kind, AND how to make a mean meatloaf! I have come to realize that she is an amazing person. Don't you agree, my husband?"

"Absolutely, Helen. I have always thought so. Whatever you say, but say it already. Anna is about to lose it here."

"Fine!" She looks disappointed at him but turns back to Anna. "Yesterday, we heard from the Insurance company. With all the testimony regarding the murder, they said that they are ruling in my favor and I, as beneficiary, will receive the full sum of Papa's policy. So, Joshua and I were talking about investments for the business and well, we want to invest in you Anna. We want to buy a Diner for you."

"Me own a Diner? But I couldn't . . ."

Henry speaks up, "Anna, we've talked about this a few times. You said that you'd like your own your own Diner when the Colonel was gone, we even discussed whether to have it in EL Dorado or here."

"Yes, but we said it would be after our little ones were off to school. Clara Beth is just getting potty trained." Anna gets off the stool that she was sitting on and goes to hug Helen. "You little dickens, you had me so frightened. This is all your idea?" She looks to Joshua for an answer.

Joshua nods, "She came up with it all by herself. What do you say Anna? Do you want to own a diner? Or two? Will you start in EL Dorado or Lawrence?

Anna smiles, "I couldn't possibly do either right now."

Everyone says at the same time. "Why not?"

"Because . . . well, um . . . I am going to have another baby!"

Now it is Henry's turn . . . to turn white.

THE END

ABOUT THE AUTHOR

Cherisse M Havlicek writes in the beautiful town of Bridgman, Michigan. She has been married for over thirty years to a now retired Chicago Police Officer. Raised in the suburbs of Chicago, she fell in love and married him in 1985. When he retired from the Police Force in 1999, they had a seven-year-old boy, Arthur, and a two-year-old girl, Alisse. They knew that they wanted to live in Michigan, where they had been coming up on weekends for many years. Cherisse has had a very varied work experience. She was a Hairdresser, an interior landscape horticulturist, a clerk at Cook County Juvenile Court, and in Michigan she worked at the daily Newspaper. There, she went from a Route manager to Single Copy manager to the top producer in the Advertising Department while raising her children, and attending their sports activities. She also helped take care of her husband's elderly mother and his disabled cousin, that lived with them, at the time.

As they became 'empty nesters', her husband was diagnosed with Lewy Body Dementia with Parkinson's. She knew that she could no longer work full time outside of the home but even part-time endeavors took her away from home too much.

In September of 2016, her grown son, Arthur, found chapter one of a book she started in high school and gave her grief about not finishing it. She wrote the next forty-five chapters in eight months and her first novel *ANNA AT LAST* was complete. She didn't stop there, though. She wrote *THE LEWIS LEGACY* while her husband had his back surgery and during his rehab. Then this installment in the A Present / Past Saga series - *JUSTICE FOR JOSHUA* was also written in 2018. She has also written a Children's Christmas story called *A SILENT NIGHT*. All of these works are now available for purchase. She, obviously, is making up for lost time and has no plans to stop.

You can connect with her on her Facebook page:
Author – Cherisse M Havlicek

Made in the USA
Middletown, DE
12 May 2019